Clementine for Christmas

DAPHNE BENEDIS-GRAB

Scholastic Press / New York

Library of Congress Control Number: 2015004644

ISBN 978-0-545-83951-8

10 9 8 7 6 5 4 3 2 1   15 16 17 18 19

Printed in U.S.A.   23
First edition, September 2015

Book design by Mary Claire Cruz

For Ainyr

Chapter 1

***

Wednesday, November 30

"Slow down," Josie's social studies teacher called as the entire class raced for the door. The final bell had just rung, and everyone was ready to leave the steamy classroom in Frost Ridge Middle School.

As the kids pushed through the door and out into the crowded hallway, Josie waited quietly at the back. She had somewhere else to be, too, but she'd rather wait a few minutes than risk getting trampled. But just then, Oscar Madison shoved past her, with Dev Gupta right behind him, his elbow smacking Josie's nose. She rubbed her face as the boys flew out of the room, not even noticing.

Students were still streaming down the hallway when Josie finally made it out of the classroom. People were clustered in groups or in pairs, talking and laughing together. Josie stayed to the side of the hall and made her way to the sixth grade locker alcove. She packed up her stuff, put on her big blue down jacket, and headed for the exit. There was a slight spring in her step by the time she finally pushed through the heavy metal doors of the school and out into the biting cold of the late November afternoon.

"I love your coat," Aisha King called right behind Josie.

Josie turned automatically—but of course popular Aisha wasn't talking to her. Josie wasn't exactly setting the fashion scene on fire with her puffy coat. Aisha had been talking to Gabby Chavez, a Frost Ridge fashion icon with her sleek, glittery outfits that all the girls tried to imitate. Gabby was also smart and beautiful, with glowing bronze skin and silky black curls. But Josie thought the true key to Gabby's popularity was the way she smiled at a person like she'd never met anyone more fascinating in her life. Gabby had once beamed at Josie like that, when Josie had picked up a pen Gabby had dropped, and that grin had lit up Josie's whole day. Whatever it was, Gabby was a sixth grade celebrity, always surrounded by a group of adoring admirers. Pretty much the opposite of Josie.

But that was okay. Josie wasn't into crowds, anyway. She shrugged it off and headed down the ice-crusted sidewalk, snowflakes landing softly on her cheeks as she walked. Frost Ridge was a small town tucked into the side of a gently sloping mountain. The west side of town overlooked the valley below and the east side viewed the peaks of more impressive neighboring mountains. It didn't take long to walk from the school to Main Street, where stores and restaurants lined the wide sidewalk leading up to the big town square. Josie inhaled deeply as she passed Snickerdoodle's. The bakery always smelled like a delicious combination of chocolate, cinnamon, and fresh-baked bread. Josie debated stopping in for one of their signature treats, a rich butter cookie coated with sugar and cinnamon, but she was already running late. Josie was eager to get to Frost Ridge County Hospital, where she volunteered almost every day, performing short skits and songs for the sick kids staying on the pediatric ward.

But she had one stop to make on her way. She turned off Main Street onto Dandelion Drive. All the streets in town, except for Main Street, were named after flowers, which was kind of funny for a town in the mountains of northern New York, where gardens bloomed less than two months of the year.

Josie walked up the path to the small gray and burgundy house that she and her mom had lived in with her grandparents for the past five years. The minute she opened the front door, she was tackled by an exuberant dog.

"I missed you, too, Clementine," Josie cooed to her beloved pet, kneeling down so she could hug her. Clementine was a mix, but she was mostly Shiba Inu, with a tan coat, a creamy white belly, soft pointed ears, and a fluffy curlicue of a tail.

Clementine was so overcome at their reunion that she yipped and danced around for a moment before snuggling close and licking Josie on the chin. Josie scratched behind Clementine's ears, the way her dog loved, and Clementine wriggled with contentment.

"You'd think we kept her locked in a closet all day," Josie's grandfather said as he made his way into the entry hall, leaning heavily on his cane.

"I know you spoil her when I'm gone," Josie teased, standing up to give her grandfather a hug, too.

"It's really coming down out there, isn't it?" her grandfather asked, patting her back and then peering out the window next to the front door. The snow was falling thick and fast.

"Yeah, it doesn't look like it's going to stop," Josie said.

"Make sure you wear a hat," Josie's grandmother said as she walked into the hallway.

"Grandma, that's cheating!" Josie cried, pointing at her grandmother. She was wearing a red sweater with candy canes dancing across the front. Every year her grandmother knit everyone in the family matching Christmas sweaters. By now they had quite a collection that they wore all through the holiday season—the candy canes were from two years earlier. But the family rule was that they had to wait until December first for any of their Christmas sweaters (as well as the vast collection of Christmas carol CDs and decorations) to come out of storage.

Her grandmother smoothed back a wisp of hair that had fallen out of her bun and smiled at Josie. "I just couldn't wait," she admitted.

Josie had to laugh at that. Her grandparents were like giddy little kids in the weeks leading up to Christmas, which was one of the many things Josie loved about living with them. Her grandparents had come from Vietnam to America when they were young to flee from the war. Josie believed they were probably the happiest people she knew, appreciating everything about their lives in America. And that was never truer than at Christmastime.

"Okay, I guess it's close enough," Josie said. "And don't worry, I have a hat, Grandma." She held up the bright green cap with earflaps that had been in her

Christmas stocking last year. Her grandmother seemed to spend most of the year knitting gifts for Christmas. "I just need to get Clementine's stuff." Josie set her backpack on the floor next to the dresser that held the family's large collection of gloves, scarves, and hats, as well as Clementine's supplies. Josie fished a leash out of the top drawer and snapped it onto Clementine's collar. Then she slipped a warm pink doggy coat over Clementine's round middle. "Ready, girl?" she asked.

Clementine barked in agreement. She always seemed to understand Josie perfectly.

"I'm making chicken curry for dinner," her grandmother said. "The one with lemongrass and sweet potatoes." Her grandmother's yummy dinners were another one of the things Josie loved about living with them. And she knew the help from her grandparents made it much easier for her mom to work her full-time job at the post office.

"I won't be late for that," Josie promised. Clementine bobbed next to her, eager to get going.

"You two have a good time," her grandfather said, holding open the door.

"Thanks, Grandpa," Josie said as she and Clementine headed out into the wintry afternoon.

"And don't work too hard," he added before closing the door behind them.

"It's not really work, is it, Clem?" Josie asked as they started down the street. Clementine trotted next to her, and Josie felt a rush of love for her dog. Five years ago, on Christmas Eve, when her father was on the verge of losing his battle with cancer, Josie had found a small tan puppy in a box next to a Dumpster behind the drugstore. Clementine had whined fearfully when Josie came close enough to see that her fur was scraggly and her paw had been injured. Josie had her own crushing pain to bear, and it lifted just the tiniest bit when she saw how much Clementine needed her. Something in Josie had healed while she cared for her new dog, and now, seeing Clementine, her fur shiny and her bark happy as she pranced about, made Josie happier than anything. Clementine had truly been the best Christmas gift ever.

Clementine was a special dog. Of course, all dogs were special, that was a given. But Clementine had a sixth sense that told her when people were upset. She had stayed close to Josie's grandmother after her grandfather's hip surgery, snuggling next to her at night and sitting at her feet while she had long, anxious phone calls with their insurance company.

When Josie's mother was worried about cutbacks at work, Clementine had stayed glued to her side. And whenever Josie felt bad about not being invited to a party or about a test that hadn't gone so well, Clementine was right there, ready to cuddle. Which was the best cure for any kind of problem, at least in Josie's mind.

And the Frost Ridge hospital seemed to feel that way, too. That was why Clementine was volunteering there as well. She was one of the founding members of the hospital's Canine Visitation Program, where trained dogs were brought in to visit patients.

Josie and Clementine turned onto Buttercup Avenue. Up ahead the bright lights of the hospital shone through the falling snow, and a minute later Josie led Clementine though the first set of automatic doors. She paused to stomp snow off her boots and brush away the small drifts that had gathered on Clementine's back before walking into the bustling hospital lobby.

"Hey there, Josie," Ms. Nunez, the security guard, said.

"Hi," Josie said, unzipping her coat so she wouldn't get sweaty on the walk to the volunteer room. Unlike Josie's home, which was kept at a chilly sixty-eight degrees to save on heating costs, this building always felt like a warm summer day.

Josie walked briskly down the beige hallway, past posters sharing health tips and hospital information, keeping her head down as she went. Aside from Ms. Nunez and a few doctors in the intensive care unit, Josie didn't know the staff outside the peds ward. And since the ward was the one place besides home where she was truly comfortable, she got there as fast as she could. Though she did always take one turn out of her way to avoid the ICU, the only section of the hospital that could still make her sad.

Josie got out of the elevator on the second floor. The walls were covered in bright murals of jungle animals and fairy-tale characters, soft chairs and toy baskets sat in the waiting area, and a big bookshelf held rows of donated books for kids of all ages. Josie had officially arrived at the peds ward. She headed straight for the nurse's station.

"Want a cookie?" Nurse Joe asked, holding up a box from Snickerdoodle's.

"Thanks." Josie happily accepted a big cinnamon cookie, which she crunched down on, the sugar and cinnamon melting on her tongue.

"How are things in your world today?" Nurse Joe asked. He was wearing scrubs printed with barnyard animals, and a matching cap covered his short dread-locks. Nurse Joe, who had dark brown skin and a wide grin at the ready, was a favorite on the ward. He used silly voices to put younger patients at ease and explained things carefully to older ones, making sure they understood exactly what was happening with their treatment.

"I'm excited about the holiday season starting tomorrow," Josie said.

"I hear that," Nurse Joe said, putting up a hand for a high five.

Josie slapped his palm, then she and Clementine headed down the hall.

"Hey, guys," Charlie, an adult volunteer, said, stopping so that Clementine and his dog, Gus, could sniff each other. Gus, who had a black-and-white spotted coat and long ears, was another enthusiastic canine volunteer.

After the humans and dogs said their hellos, Charlie and Gus moved on to visit patients while Josie and Clementine continued to the volunteer room.

"Hi, Josie," Ed Santamaria said when she walked in. He was standing in front of the full-length mirror adjusting his curly red wig. He was clearly in clown mode, with baggy polka-dot pants and bright purple suspenders to go with the wig.

"Hi, Josie," echoed Jade Chen. She was inside the costume closet and her voice was muffled.

"Hey," Josie said, greeting her fellow volunteers and letting Clementine off her leash so she could say hi, too. Ed and Jade were students at the high school. They performed skits and songs but didn't participate in the Canine Visitation Program, so they always enjoyed snuggling Clementine, who was more than happy to oblige.

Jade emerged from the closet in a red flannel footed onesie and sleeping cap pulled over her long black hair. "I thought I'd try something new today," she said, petting Clementine and then shoving Ed playfully away from the mirror so she could get the tassel of her hat just right. "I'm going to be Suzie Sleeps-a-lot."

"Sounds like a snore," Ed said, and Josie and Jade both groaned.

"Come on, Josie, you think I'm funny, right?" Ed asked with big, pleading eyes, his hands clasped at his chest. Clearly he was getting into his clown character. Ed and Jade were both members of the high school drama club and wanted to be actors when they graduated, but not Josie. She only liked performing here for the kids and their families.

"Sorry," Josie said, laughing.

Even though she was the youngest volunteer, she never felt left out. The others included her in all their conversations, and, until last week, Josie had gone around the ward with a partner. But Josie's partner, Ainyr Swift, had stopped working at the hospital because she was too busy with college applications. Josie was going to miss the fun they had together. She could sing by herself, but she was hoping to find another partner soon.

"See you, Josie," Ed said.

Jade blew a kiss as they walked out to begin their rounds.

The door closed behind them, and Josie headed for the costume closet. She was in the mood for something silly, maybe the fried egg outfit or the cowgirl dress with matching rhinestone-studded boots. As she stepped into the closet, she couldn't help gazing at the rack holding her favorite costumes: velvety elf suits, plush Santa coats, and shimmery angel gowns. Performing for the kids was fun year-round, but it was best during the month leading up to Christmas. The month that would begin tomorrow. And Josie could hardly wait.

For now, Josie pulled on the cowgirl costume, stepped into the sparkly boots, and grabbed the big ten-gallon hat that went with it. She took a moment to put her hair in a ponytail so it wouldn't get in her face while she performed. Josie always wished she'd inherited her mother's thick black hair that cascaded down her shoulders, kind of like Gabby Chavez and her mane of curls. But while Josie got her tan skin and brown eyes from the Asian side of her family, her thin, blah brown hair came from her dad.

When she came out of the closet dressed and ready to go, she saw that Ms. D'Amato, the volunteer coordinator, had come in and was petting Clementine.

"Josie," Ms. D'Amato said. "How are you?" The volunteer coordinator was normally chipper, but today the bounce was gone from her voice. Clementine noticed and pressed her furry body against Ms. D'Amato's legs.

"I'm good, thanks," Josie said, turning the cowboy hat in her hands. "How are you?"

Ms. D'Amato seemed to sag in her red high heels. "Well, I'm afraid I have some bad news," she said.

The words *bad news* made Josie's stomach clench, and she was suddenly gripping the hat so hard, the brim bent back in her hands. Clementine was by her side in seconds, leaning gently against her.

"It's about the Christmas Festival," Ms. D'Amato said. The Festival took place every Christmas Eve and was the big finish to a month of holiday fun. It was a jubilant show with skits, musical numbers, and a big carol sing-along, and it gave kids who were in the hospital over the holidays a fun celebration with their families. Children who had chronic illnesses that took them in and out of the hospital throughout the year came, and members of the community, including the town council and mayor, were also invited so that the whole lower auditorium was packed for hours of Christmasy fun. Ms. D'Amato and everyone else knew it was Josie's favorite event of the year, though none of them, not even her mom, knew the exact reason why.

"Is there a problem?" Josie asked, still twisting the hat.

"The problem is that there's no one to organize it," Ms. D'Amato said. "Olivia Bakir in admissions has always done it, but she's retiring next week and moving to New Mexico. She doesn't have time to find volunteers to perform and to supervise the rehearsals."

"And there's no one else who wants to do it?" Josie asked. There was no way that could be true.

But Ms. D'Amato shook her head. "I'm afraid not," she said. "Everyone's just so busy since the budget was cut."

"But what about the kids?" Josie asked, her voice shrill in her ears. "They'll be so disappointed."

"I know," Ms. D'Amato said, the corners of her mouth turning down. "I wish there was something I could do, but I'm overextended as it is."

Josie knew how hard the volunteer coordinator worked, often staying late and coming in on weekends to make sure everyone had what they needed to entertain the patients. But there had to be someone, anyone, who could take over the Festival.

"I'm sorry, Josie," Ms. D'Amato said. She straightened up, ready to head back out. "I know how much the Festival means to you. We'll all miss it this year."

Josie couldn't let this happen.

The last thing she wanted was to have to approach people she didn't know and ask them to participate in the Festival. And the thought of running rehearsals made her feel lightheaded, like she might pass out onto the worn sofa on the far side of the room. But there was no other option, not if she wanted to save her beloved Festival.

So Josie stood as tall as she could in her cowboy boots and spoke with all the confidence she could muster. "I'll do it," she said. "I'll be in charge of the Festival."

Chapter 2

Thursday, December 1

"Morning, sweetie," Oscar's mom said, pausing to give him a kiss on the top of his head as she headed for the coffeemaker on the counter.

"Hi, Mom," Oscar said. He had been telling her since he was nine that he was too old for kissing. But it made his mom happy and since it was just the two of them in the kitchen, Oscar decided to let it go. He had gotten a bowl out of the cabinet and was standing in front of the pantry trying to decide what kind of cereal to have. The choices were pretty grim because his mom was really into healthy food. He could have puffed corn that turned into soggy paper-like balls after three seconds in milk, or whole grain cereal that tasted like wood pellets. With a sigh, Oscar selected the puffed corn.

"Tonight we're going to—oh, I can't believe this," his mom said, her voice going from cheerful to irritated in less than two seconds. "Your father forgot to turn the coffeemaker on last night. Again." His mom was unable to start her day without at least two cups of coffee.

"This is going to make me late," she grumbled as she stabbed at the machine's on button. She was already dressed for work as the manager of Green Apple Grocery, the town supermarket, and Oscar knew how important it was that she arrive on time. "Your father promised he'd make sure the timer was set."

Oscar quietly got out the milk and said nothing. His parents often argued over things like a forgotten timer, and it always got worse around this time of year. Something about the holidays put everyone in his house on edge, which was why Oscar was the one kid in town who didn't like Christmas. At all.

Oscar poured the cereal into his bowl. Maybe his dad would run late and not get to the kitchen until his mom had left. But a moment later, his dad strode in, adjusting his tie, ready for his day of work at Frost Ridge Bank, where he did something that involved sitting behind a desk. Oscar never really understood when his dad explained his job—something about finance and analysis—and he secretly suspected no one else did, either.

"Good morning," his dad said, all cheery, the way he often was first thing in the morning.

"Morning, Dad," Oscar said.

"You forgot to set the timer on the coffeemaker," Oscar's mom said.

"Sorry," his dad said, in a tone that did not sound sorry at all. Or cheery. His shoulders sagged as he went over to the counter.

"It's on now," Oscar's mom said sharply.

Oscar was pouring the milk over his cereal, but somehow he misjudged things, and suddenly milk flooded out of his bowl and pooled on the polished wooden table.

"Watch it," Oscar's dad snapped.

"I—" Oscar began.

"Don't yell at Oscar," his mother said, in a voice that sounded a lot like yelling. "Accidents happen."

"He's twelve, and that's too old for an accident with milk," his father said. "Stop making excuses for him."

"I'm not making excuses," his mother huffed. "And you need to stop crushing his self-esteem."

"What does self-esteem have to do with milk?" his father asked, throwing out his arms as though over-whelmed by how absurd his mother was being.

It was always at this point, when the arm throwing happened, that his mother's face got red and her voice rose an octave.

"Don't act like everything I say is stupid!" she snarled.

And this was the point when Oscar needed to escape. He shoved his cereal bowl into the sink and nearly ran out of the room. Not that his parents noticed—they were too busy shouting at each other. Oscar's chest burned the way it always did when they fought, and he sped out of the house.

As soon as he got outside, he realized he'd forgotten his hat and gloves. The frigid morning air bit into his hands, but he shoved them deep in his pockets and jogged to school, his stomach growling and his fingers clenching into tight fists.

* * * 🦴 * * *

"HEY, O," OSCAR'S friend Dev called.

"Hey," Oscar said as he dodged through the crowded hallway at school. He and Dev had played soccer together in the fall, and Dev was the kind of guy who was always friendly to everyone. Probably because his parents weren't fighting with each other all the time and most likely sat around the breakfast table talking instead of screaming. Dev would never get what things were like in Oscar's house. Oscar tried to smile.

"Did you do the English homework?" Dev asked, falling in step next to Oscar.

With a sinking feeling in his gut, Oscar thought of the homework set out on the hall dresser so he wouldn't forget it. And still sitting on the dresser because he'd been in such a rush to get out of the house. But Dev didn't need to know about that.

Oscar managed a nonchalant shrug. "No, I didn't get to it," he said.

Dev looked concerned. "Didn't you get detention last week for missing too much homework?"

"It's no big deal," Oscar said.

"Whatever you say," Dev said, smiling and cheerful again. "Are you going out for basketball?" The Frost Ridge Middle School had a pretty good team, and Oscar was eager for tryouts next week. Last year he'd scored more baskets than anyone else on the fifth grade team, and he was hoping to continue that streak.

"Yeah, definitely," he said.

"Cool, me too," Dev said as they walked into English class.

"You don't belong on the team." It was Frank Harrison looking right at Oscar. Frank had scored the second-highest number of baskets last year. Everyone knew that Frank had been held back when he was little, so he was a year older—and a year bigger and a year stronger—than all the other boys in sixth grade, which was a big advantage when it came to sports. And when it came to being a total jerk.

Oscar felt his fingers slowly curl into fists. "You're just jealous of my skills," he said to Frank, stepping closer to the taller boy. It had been deeply satisfying to beat Frank on the court last year, and he was already looking forward to doing it again.

"Everyone, sit down, please," their English teacher, Ms. Keller, said as the bell rang.

Out of the corner of his eye, Oscar saw Dev shoot him a look as he slipped into his seat behind perfect Gabby Chavez. Oscar knew he should sit, too, but somehow he couldn't make his legs move.

"No one wants you on the team," Frank said, his words smooth like velvet, as if he'd been planning to say them for a while. "Because you're a ball hog who cares more about his own stats than a win for the team."

Oscar's fist smashed into Frank's face before he even realized what he was doing. Pain shot down his arm and his fist burned. But not as hot as the burning in his chest.

Frank shouted, then shoved Oscar so hard, he hit the wall behind him, his head smacking against the doorjamb. Oscar ignored the throbbing in his skull as he lunged at Frank, taking the bigger boy down in a heap. Kids were shrieking and Ms. Keller was yelling, but Oscar couldn't stop. He cocked his fist back and was about to hit Frank again when someone grabbed him from behind.

"Dude, stop," Dev said, his voice a bit shaky as he pulled Oscar away from Frank.

Frank was up and Ms. Keller had his arm. "To the principal, *now*," she said, eyes blazing.

Oscar sagged in Dev's grip, the fight seeping out of him and leaving behind a stomach-curdling sense of shame.

"OSCAR, THIS IS a disappointment," Ms. Antonoff said, her hands folded carefully on her big principal's desk.

Oscar shrugged, but his heart was beating a little faster than normal. This was not his first visit to the principal's office, with its motivational posters and comfortable chairs that tried hard to cover up the fact that the room was a punishment factory. And Oscar was not excited to hear what his punishment was going to be this time.

"The last time we spoke, I believe you promised to control that temper of yours and start getting your work done, is that correct?" the principal asked in the no-nonsense voice they probably taught her in principal school.

Oscar shrugged again.

"Answer me with the spoken word, Mr. Madison," Ms. Antonoff said in a quiet but deadly voice that made Oscar sit up straight. They probably taught that in principal school, too.

"Yes, ma'am," Oscar said. Maybe being polite could get him out of this. Too bad he hadn't thought of it sooner.

"And you have broken that promise," Ms. Antonoff stated.

Oscar slumped down again. No amount of politeness was going to help him now. "Yeah, sorry," he said.

"While I appreciate your sincere and heartfelt regret," the principal said, reaching into her desk and taking out a folder, "I'm afraid this infraction will require more from you."

Great. Now Oscar had given his parents some-thing else to argue about.

"You'll be suspended for one day," Ms. Antonoff said.

"But—" Oscar sputtered.

Ms. Antonoff held up a hand. "As I was saying, you'll be suspended, as is the consequence for strik-ing another student. But you'll also need to make reparations."

Oscar had no idea what reparations were, but he could tell he was not going to like them. At all.

"You'll do volunteer work. There's a wonderful program at the pediatric ward of the hospital," Ms. Antonoff said, handing him an information sheet about the program. "You'll go three times a week and every Saturday afternoon for the month of December to help them put on performances and visit with the sick children."

There was no way.

"Sorry, I can't. I'm trying out for basketball, and there's practice every day after school," Oscar said. "And I don't even like little kids."

"First of all, you lost the privilege of trying out for basketball when you chose to use violence in school," Ms. Antonoff said. "And second of all, if you're going to act like a little kid, you may as well spend time with them."

Oscar couldn't believe it. He'd been looking forward to basketball for ages. Now, not only would he lose it, he would be stuck at the hospital, surrounded by sick, miserable kids for an entire month.

"I'm not doing it," he said, his voice louder than he had intended.

But Ms. Antonoff just raised one eyebrow. "You don't actually have a choice in the matter," she said crisply. "And I suspect in the end you'll enjoy it."

She held Oscar's gaze, and the look in her eyes sent a clear message: The whistle had blown and Oscar had lost.

"The volunteers sing and put on skits for the children, and there's a festival on Christmas Eve that your family can attend," Ms. Antonoff went on cheerfully, knowing that she had won. "It's really very special."

It sounded a lot more like a complete nightmare.

"I don't even like Christmas," Oscar muttered dismally.

Ms. Antonoff stood up. "Well, then a whole world of wonder awaits you, Mr. Madison. Off you go, to discover the magic of helping people and of Christmas."

Oscar trudged toward the door of her office like a prisoner being forced off a plank. Though right now shark-infested waters sounded pretty good compared to what he was facing.

As he sank down in a chair in the outside office across from a glaring Frank, Oscar decided it was official. He hated Christmas. Nothing could ever change his mind about that.

Chapter 3

❦

Thursday, December 1

"I can't believe we have another essay for English," Aisha said to Gabby. School had just ended, and the hallway was steamy and crowded as they slowly headed for the big doors at the front of the school, surrounded by Jasmine Davis, Isabelle Romanov, and Becky Hollis, their usual group of friends. "I wanted to go shopping this weekend, not get stuck in front of the computer writing about *The Outsiders*."

"I know," Gabby agreed. Truthfully, she didn't mind the essay. She'd really enjoyed the book, and writing about it would be kind of fun. But she'd never say that to Aisha, who made it clear that shopping trumped homework at all times.

"I bet you'll ace it, though," Aisha said, grinning at Gabby, a knowing glint in her eye.

"Totally," Jasmine agreed.

Gabby smiled and shrugged like it didn't matter that much one way or the other. After all, she cared about getting people to like her, not getting them to think she was a star student.

"I should come over to your house to work on it," Aisha said. "It would be more fun that way. And my parents promised me a new cell phone if I get my grades up."

Gabby hadn't had anyone over to her house since her family had moved to Frost Ridge the summer after fourth grade, and she planned to keep it that way. "I usually study at the library," she said, the lie easy and natural.

"Well, one day I'm finding you there," Aisha said as they finally pushed through the door and out into the frosty afternoon. Gabby would worry about that if it happened, but it wasn't likely. Gabby made it a point to know the habits of her friends, and Aisha was a lot more likely to spend her free time shopping, not studying.

As they walked down the steps of the school, their boots crunching on the salt the janitors poured on all the stairways and paths outside of school, Gabby felt a tug on her arm.

"I love your skirt," Isabelle said. "Where'd you get it?"

Gabby grinned. "Mulligans," she said.

Isabelle's brows flew up. "Seriously?"

Mulligans was a discount store in the next town over. Most of Gabby's crowd shopped at the local mall, but that wasn't in the Chavez family budget. Not that Gabby minded—when she was younger, Gabby had adored playing dress-up with the fanciest gowns and accessories she could find. Now she loved adding a bit of flair to the clothes she bought—a few sequins here or a ribbon there.

"I can't believe you found something that pretty at Mulligans," Aisha said, a brow raised as she inspected Gabby's black wool skirt. It was dotted with delicate diamond rhinestone flowers and had a silver satin ribbon sewn along the hem.

"Yeah," Gabby said. "It was on a rack with these awful polyester plaid skirts, just waiting for me to come rescue it."

"Let's go shopping together sometime," Isabelle said hopefully. She'd been pushing to spend more time with Gabby, acting like they were just on the cusp of BFF-hood. But Gabby didn't do best friends, not after Jenny. Sure, Isabelle seemed nice, but Jenny had, too, at least until she'd turned on Gabby, shredding Gabby's life apart at the seams. If Jenny could do it, so could Isabelle. Or Aisha, or Jasmine, or any of the other girls. So Gabby stuck with group socializing and casual get-togethers where no one got too close.

She gave Isabelle one of her brilliant smiles. "Maybe a bunch of us could go sometime," she said.

"Hey, Gabby, where were you yesterday?" Becky asked, jostling in to get closer to Gabby. "We missed you at yearbook."

And just like that, it was time to lie again. Gabby had missed the yearbook meeting for a medical appointment, but there was no way she was telling Becky or anyone else about that. "I had to babysit my little brothers," she said smoothly.

Yes, Gabby was good at school, being creative with clothes, and getting people to like her, but her best skill? Lying. She'd been doing it for the past year and four months, ever since the day her family had come to Frost Ridge, and never once had she been caught. The girls who called themselves her friends thought they knew her, but all they knew was what Gabby allowed them to see, and not a single thing more.

Because if they ever saw behind Gabby's facade and discovered the secret she was hiding, they would hate her, every last one of them.

Chapter 4

Friday, December 2

"Remember I'm taking Clementine to the vet for her yearly checkup this afternoon," Josie's mom said. She took a final sip of her coffee, pushed herself out of her seat in their cozy breakfast nook, and smoothed down her post office uniform. Sometimes her mom worked half days during the week, and today was one of them.

"That's right," Josie said, standing up and going to rinse out her cereal bowl. "It's a good day for it, actually. It means I can get to the hospital early this afternoon so I can start signing people up for the Festival."

"Well, good luck," her mom said. "And have I mentioned that I think you should sign yourself up and let the world hear that gorgeous voice of yours?" She had—many times.

"I'll be too busy," Josie said. Her standard excuse normally wouldn't work on her mom, but until she had several cups of coffee, she wasn't fully herself. The two of them headed for the front hall and began bundling up to face the frigid morning.

Only a few rays of sunlight slid over the mountain peaks, and Josie knew it was well below freezing. "You're lucky to stay inside," she told Clementine, who was sitting by the door as though ready to see them off.

"She sure is," her mom agreed.

Josie opened the front door, and an icy wind whipped in. "See you tonight," she said to both her mom and Clementine, then headed off to school, her mind already racing ahead to the time she would spend at the hospital.

"LOOKING GOOD," **ED** said when Josie strode out of the costume closet that afternoon. She was wearing a velour Santa suit with big black boots and a hat covered in small silver bells that jingled as she walked.

"Thanks," Josie said, straightening her hat. "I'm so glad it's time for the holiday costumes."

"Me too," Jade said with a grin. She and Ed were dressed as elves.

"I have something to ask you guys," Josie said, smoothing her red coat. "I'm kind of organizing the Christmas Festival this year, and I was hoping maybe you guys would do a skit."

She was not very good at this, but Jade and Ed were both nodding.

"For sure," Jade said. "Maybe we can do a riff on *The Nutcracker* so we can dance."

Ed's nose wrinkled. "Or something else that doesn't involve dancing," he said. Then he grinned at Josie. "But we're in for sure."

"Thanks," Josie said, her cheeks warming with pleasure. She'd managed to sign up the first act for the Festival! Hopefully this would show Ms. D'Amato that Josie was up to the task of running things. The volunteer coordinator had not been confident when Josie brought it up, but she'd agreed to let Josie try. Since the show was in the hospital auditorium, there was no need to book the space in advance—all they needed was a list of volunteers by December 20 and two rehearsals. Ms. D'Amato had said ten acts would make for a strong show, and now Josie only had nine to go—she could do that, she was sure of it. Yes, it was uncomfortable to ask for a favor, but as long as she was asking people she knew from the peds ward, it wouldn't be that bad.

"Are you going to perform?" Jade asked Josie.

Josie shook her head so sharply the bells on her hat rang out. "No, I'll be too busy organizing," she said. That wasn't the real reason, but it seemed good enough for Jade.

"Too bad," Jade said. "You have such a pretty voice."

"Thanks," Josie said, ducking her head at the compliment. She really did love to sing but not in front of people, at least not too many of them. Performing for the patients was easy because it was just one or two to a room plus a parent or sibling. It also helped that Josie wore such extravagant costumes. In her layers of crushed velveteen or satin, her face half hidden under a bright hat, Josie felt like another person, one who was brave and didn't get tongue-tied the second anyone looked at her, the way she did at school.

"We'll see you later," Jade said as she and Ed headed out.

"See you," Josie said. She wished Ainyr was here. She knew Ed and Jade would be happy to have her tag along, but they had their own routines already. Kind of like Josie had had with Ainyr. Last year they'd come up with a series of Christmas comedy sketches about an elf who kept breaking the toys she made, and the kids had loved them. Going solo just wasn't as fun, but Josie reminded herself that what mattered was cheering up the kids. She was going to meet a four-year-old boy who had come out of surgery earlier in the day, and lifting his spirits was the important thing.

"Josie, I'm glad I caught you." It was Ms. D'Amato, and Josie turned, excited to tell Ms. D'Amato that she'd found the very first act for the Festival. But when she saw who Ms. D'Amato was leading into the volunteer room, her excitement fizzled abruptly. "We have a new volunteer, and I was hoping you could show him around and then partner together."

Josie, eyes wide, looked at Oscar, the boy from English class who'd attacked another boy for no reason. He was looking right back at Josie, and she could tell he was trying not to laugh. That's when she realized how ridiculous she looked in her costume, and her cheeks heated up. "Um, okay, but I wonder if maybe Jade or Ed—"

"Great," Ms. D'Amato interrupted. "You can help Oscar get suited up and then you guys can go visit Peter." She turned to Oscar. "Oscar, Josie's usual partner just left, so this is perfect timing. I'm sure you guys will come up with some wonderful ideas together for plays and songs for the kids."

Josie was not sure of this at all.

Ms. D'Amato walked out of the room, and Oscar folded his arms across his chest. "I'm not dressing up," he informed her.

Josie gulped. "The kids really like it," she said, her voice squeaky.

Oscar shrugged. "Whatever, I'm not doing it."

"But, I mean, aren't you here to try and cheer them up? Because the costumes make them laugh."

"Yeah, I bet," Oscar said in a snide voice as he took in her costume a second time. "But I'm not going to make a fool of myself just to get some kid to laugh at me."

Josie drew herself up to her full height, which had the unfortunate effect of making the bells on her hat ring out. "They don't laugh at me; they laugh *with* me," she said haughtily. At least she hoped she sounded haughty.

"I doubt it, if you go in there dressed like that," Oscar said.

Josie was not going to take this lying down. Oscar might get by at school by intimidating people, but this was her place and she wasn't going to allow him to ruin it.

"It's obvious you have no idea what you're talking about," she informed him tartly. "And you came here to help so—"

"I didn't come here to help anyone," Oscar interrupted. He spit the word *help* like it was some kind of contagious disease.

"Then, what are you doing here?" Josie asked.

Oscar sighed. "The school is forcing me to make repercussions for getting in a fight," he said. "So I'm here as a punishment."

Josie wasn't sure how working at the hospital would make repercussions, but she had bigger things to worry about now. It was getting late and Peter was waiting. "Fine, come on, then," she said. "You can start wearing a costume tomorrow. For now you can just perform with me. I'm going to sing silly Christmas songs, like 'Grandma Got Run Over by a Reindeer,' and do a dance to go along with them." It would be too much to do a skit today, especially since Oscar wouldn't dress up, but at least they could sing.

Oscar looked pale. "Yeah, there's no way I'm doing any of that," he said.

Josie put her hands on her hips. "So what *are* you going to do?" she asked. "Because it sounds like the school will be mad if you don't do anything."

Oscar sighed as though she was the one being difficult. "I'll observe," he said finally. "That's what people do their first day on the job."

"Fine," Josie huffed, turning and heading out of the room. The last thing she wanted was Oscar observing her, but there wasn't any more time to argue, not when Peter was expecting them. Once they got to a room he'd probably join in, anyway— after all, if he had to be there as punishment he couldn't just stand there while she did all the work. At least she hoped he couldn't.

"Hey there, Josie," Dr. Scott called as she walked past. She was wearing Santa-printed scrubs underneath her doctor's jacket and had a candy cane pin that lit up.

Josie greeted the nurses as she passed their station, which was now decorated with a tiny Christmas tree, statues of angels, reindeer, and elves, and a menorah with lightbulbs that would turn on one-by-one for each day of Hanukkah.

When they walked into room 212, a little boy with a bandage around one arm sat up in the bed and let out a squeal of delight. "Mama, look who came to see me!"

His mom looked like she hadn't slept in days, but she gave them a smile.

"I'm Josie, and this is Oscar," Josie said. "Want us to sing you some Christmas songs?"

"Yes!" Peter shouted.

Peter looked thrilled, but Josie couldn't help being slightly distracted by Oscar, who was scuffing his sneakers along the floor. She started in with "Jingle Bells," hoping someone would join in, but Peter lay back, probably still fatigued from his surgery, and his mom stroked his forehead and stayed silent. The worst part was Oscar smirking like Josie was some kind of basket case.

"Peter, what do you want Santa to bring you this year?" Josie asked when she was done with the song.

Peter launched into a list, and Josie nodded and made small noises of approval. And tried to ignore Oscar rolling his eyes.

"Sing more," Peter said after he'd carefully explained to Josie how badly he needed a pet dinosaur.

Again, this was something that Josie normally loved. But somehow launching into "All I Want for Christmas (Is My Two Front Teeth)" with a silly lisp felt forced, especially when she added in her dance. In fact, she was so on edge under Oscar's critical gaze that she even messed up the last verse. Peter didn't seem to mind, but Josie minded. A lot.

After joking around with Peter for a few more minutes, Josie stalked out, bells ringing loudly.

"Can we go—" Oscar began, but Josie whirled around and glared at him.

"You can't ever do that again," she said.

Oscar raised his hands and stepped back. "What? I was just watching, to get the hang of it."

"Really?" Josie asked, hands on hips. "So you'll be wearing a costume and singing with me next time, instead of making me do everything?"

The corners of Oscar's mouth turned up. "Oh, no," he said smoothly. "It's much too complicated to do after watching only once. I'm going to have to observe a lot more, maybe even a whole month, before I'll be ready to do that."

Josie was fuming, but she had no comeback for that. So she turned, nearly falling in her slippery Santa boots, and stalked down the hall, Oscar trailing behind.

Josie blinked back tears as she passed the Christmas tree nestled between two rooms, its colored lights warm and bright. This was *her* place and Christmas was *her* season.

And there was no way she was going to let Oscar ruin either one.

Chapter 5

Saturday, December 3

"You said you'd pay it." Oscar's mother's icy tone stopped Oscar in his tracks just outside the kitchen. Oscar's mom had a low, musical voice, and she often sang as she cooked or tidied up around the house. But lately there hadn't been any singing, just this new, bitter voice arguing with his dad.

"I have no memory of that," his father said sharply. "Paying the bills is your responsibility. That's what we agreed the last time this happened."

His parents were starting their day with a fight. Again.

"This bill is for your car repair!" his mother said, raising her voice. "How is that my responsibility?"

"Stop shouting. It's uncivilized," his father barked. When Oscar was little, his dad had loved teaching him new words like *responsible* and *uncivilized*, showing Oscar the dictionary like it was a tool for magic.

He had never mentioned that these words could be used to attack someone in a fight.

"You're the one shouting, and it's going to upset Oscar," his mother pretty much yelled.

Oscar was not going to get dragged into this. The only thing worse than his parents fighting about him was them fighting about him when he was in the room. Although his stomach was growling because he hadn't eaten much dinner last night, thanks to the fight his parents had about dirty breakfast dishes left in the sink, Oscar walked quietly to the front hall. Now his parents were yelling so loudly he could have stomped past while singing one of Josie's stupid songs and no one would have noticed. Oscar slid his feet into his winter boots, which chafed a little since he wasn't wearing socks. But he wasn't going to take the time to go upstairs now. Instead, he just put on his coat, hat, and gloves, and grabbed the wallet out of his backpack that he'd left in the front hall since Friday afternoon. Normally, his mother would have nagged him about it, but she'd been too busy fighting with his dad. Which was typical for the Christmas season in Oscar's house.

The sun was newly risen, making the fresh blanket of snow on Oscar's front yard glitter. The whipping wind, however, was bone cold, so Oscar huddled down into his coat and picked up his pace. His neighbors had already begun to decorate for Christmas. The Barrs had a big Santa sleigh, complete with reindeer and twinkling lights. Old Mrs. Watson had colored lights strung through the bushes in her yard as well as candles in every window of the house. They were the electric kind that went on automatically each night. The Jordans had a family of snow-people in their yard, all wearing Santa hats and holding big plastic candy canes. And on the corner, the Holts had elves surrounding a big Rudolph, whose nose shone bright red. Oscar couldn't help thinking Josie would have loved it, but the whole thing made his empty stomach turn. He kept his gaze on the sidewalk in front of him as he walked the last two blocks into town.

Most stores on Main Street hadn't opened yet, but the lights were on in Danny's Diner and Snickerdoodle's. Oscar and his parents ate at Danny's on Saturday nights, a family tradition Oscar didn't want to think about now as they hadn't gone in weeks, so he headed to Snickerdoodle's. All the businesses on Main Street were ready for Christmas, with blinking lights and cheery Christmas window displays that only worsened Oscar's mood. He averted his eyes from the elaborate gingerbread house that sat at the front of

Snickerdoodle's, as well as the tree in one corner trimmed with bakery-themed ornaments, like mini utensils and gingerbread people. His boots scuffed on the glossy wood floor as he headed up to the big display case that held newly baked breads and pastries.

"Hey, Oscar," Keri Joel said. She and her husband, Campbell, had opened the bakery before Oscar was born and had known him and every other kid in town since they were babies.

"Good morning," Oscar said, trying to sound polite. Keri and Campbell were really nice, the kind of people who snuck kids chocolate chip cookies when their parents weren't looking. He didn't want to take his wretched mood out on her.

"Where are your folks?" Keri asked, glancing behind him. She was wearing a red-and-green-striped apron and her baker's hat was red and lined with white felt like a Santa hat.

Oscar frowned at the outfit and the question. "They're doing stuff at home," he said. Keri was now looking at him sympathetically, which made his skin all itchy. "Can I get a muffin?"

"Sure, sweetie, what kind?" Keri asked.

It was a normal question, but Oscar felt a flash of irritation. "Any kind is fine," he said. He'd tried to keep his voice even, but Keri glanced at him before reaching into a display case and plucking a muffin off a platter.

"How does a gingerbread muffin sound?" she asked. "A little bite of Christmas for you."

It was about the worst choice she could have made, but Oscar was too hungry to argue. "Great," he said, handing her two dollars from his wallet.

Keri waved it away. "Don't worry, it's on the house," she said.

Oscar stuffed the money into the tip jar, which made Keri smile. "You're a generous soul," she told him.

No one had ever accused Oscar of being generous before, but he just said thanks and headed for the door.

"Why don't you eat here where it's warm?" Keri said, the sympathetic look back on her face.

"I have to meet a friend," Oscar lied. He had an hour before he had to start his volunteer shift at the hospital, and nowhere to be and nothing to do, but he knew that if he sat, Keri would come chat with him, no doubt asking about stuff Oscar was in no mood to talk about. Like home or school or what he did after school. Basically everything in his life was stuff he was in no mood to talk about.

But after eating his muffin, Oscar was cold and bored. Every place was closed, he didn't feel like seeing any of his friends, and there was no way he was going home, so finally Oscar headed to the only place he could think of.

· · · 🦴 · · ·

IT WAS FORTY minutes before he was supposed to start his Saturday shift, so Oscar was surprised to see Josie when he walked into the volunteer room. And she looked equally surprised to see him.

"What are you doing here?" she asked, like Oscar was a moldy piece of bread she had discovered in a corner.

"What do you think?" he snapped. He had been shocked to find someone from his class working in the hospital and then dismayed when the volunteer coordinator announced they'd be working together. At school, Josie was quiet, but here she was some kind of nut with her crazy costumes and the embarrassing songs she sang. Working in the hospital was bad enough on its own without getting paired up with someone this weird.

"Well, you're early, so I don't know," Josie snapped back.

Weird and hostile. It was strange how she was always so quiet at school but then was so loud and difficult here. Clearly the hospital brought out the worst in everyone.

"You must be Oscar."

Oscar turned and nearly jumped back when he saw two elves emerging from the costume closet. "Um, yeah," he said.

"I'm Jade, and this is Ed," the elf said, reaching out a green-gloved hand.

Oscar shook her hand hesitantly, the glove soft against his skin.

"I think I saw you yesterday," Ed said. "When we were singing carols in the lounge. Are you ready to join in today?"

"Yes," Josie said loudly as Oscar shook his head and glared at her. "He's ready to pull his own weight now that he's seen what to do."

Oscar glared at her; he had no plans to pull anything.

The two elves exchanged a glance.

"Is everything okay, Josie?" Jade asked.

"Fine, thanks," Josie said with a smile that was clearly forced.

"We're around if you want to join us later," Ed said. Then the two elves headed out.

"Those are two of the high school volunteers," Josie said as the door shut behind them. "There are only a few of us to entertain all the kids. It's not enough, which is why you need to help out. Plus, I can't do skits on my own."

"Maybe I can carry something for you guys, like a prop," Oscar offered. That much he was willing to do.

"That's not a help at all!" Josie exclaimed. "We don't even use props."

"What about this?" Oscar asked, picking up a big plastic candy cane.

"I can carry that myself," Josie retorted, rolling her eyes.

"Well, I—" Oscar began, but then a furry missile shot out of the closet and straight into his arms. Oscar started in surprise as the tan dog reached up and licked him on the nose.

"Sorry, she likes meeting new people," Josie said, reaching out to take the dog. But the dog snuggled close to Oscar, and Oscar found that he wasn't willing to let go of her just yet.

"No problem," he said, shifting the dog in his arms so he could pet her. The dog's fur was feathery and soft. "What's a dog doing in the hospital?"

"Didn't you notice dogs here yesterday?" Josie asked unhelpfully.

"Obviously not," Oscar said, more nicely than he wanted to since he didn't want to upset the dog.

"There's a program where dogs can come in to cheer up patients," Josie said.

"Don't they bring in germs?" Oscar asked, interested despite himself.

"They only see approved patients," Josie said. "And if they get on a patient's bed, the nurse puts down a sheet. Plus, when we bring our dogs in, we clean their feet and stuff."

"So this dog is yours?" Oscar asked. He'd started petting the dog on her head, but she wiggled around until he was scratching behind her ears, which she seemed to really like. Her tongue was out as she panted happily, licking his hand every now and again as if to tell him to keep on scratching.

Josie's face softened as she gazed at the dog. "Yeah, that's Clementine," she said. But then her eyes narrowed. "And she helps out with patients a lot more than you do."

Oscar scowled at her.

"Whatever, I'm going to get dressed," Josie said. She disappeared into the closet.

Oscar sat down on the sofa and settled Clementine on his lap. She was warm and her weight felt just right. For the first time in days Oscar's insides unclenched just the littlest bit. He rubbed Clementine's velvety ears and leaned back with a sigh.

A few minutes later, Josie appeared wearing a reindeer outfit that included a big red bow under her chin and a pair of jingle bell–covered antlers. In other words, looking completely ridiculous.

Clearly she didn't see it that way, though. She stood in front of the mirror adjusting the antlers at a jaunty angle. When she had it right she picked up a red-and-green leash from the table and called Clementine, who hopped off Oscar's lap. His legs felt cold now that she was gone.

"So what are you going to do?" Josie asked again, like a song stuck on repeat.

But then Oscar had a flash of inspiration. "I can walk Clementine around to visit with patients while you sing and stuff," Oscar said. It was the perfect solution: Josie could do the embarrassing stuff while he stood in the background and let people pet Clementine.

But Josie's mouth was all scrunched up like she'd just bitten into a crab apple. "I can do that," she said.

But then the little dog barked and walked toward Oscar as far as the leash would allow.

"She likes you," Josie said, sounding more stunned than Oscar cared for.

"She has good taste," he informed her.

"Fine," Josie said with a sigh. "You can take her around when we visit with the kids today. But next time you have to sing or do a skit with me."

There was no way Oscar was going to agree to that, but Josie handed over the leash without waiting for him to reply and led the way out of the volunteer room.

"Hi, Josie," said a woman holding the leash of a small fuzzy dog who stopped to sniff Clementine.

"Hi, Eliza," Josie said. "This is Oscar." Her voice was a lot less enthusiastic as she said his name. "He's volunteering here, too."

"Nice to meet you, Oscar," Eliza said with a warm smile. "This is Jeremy. We come in twice a week to visit."

"Nice to meet you, too," Oscar said, rubbing his foot on the smooth linoleum floor.

"I was wondering," Josie said to Eliza. "Can you be in the Christmas Festival this year? Everyone loved it last year when you and your husband performed that carol medley."

"Oh, I wish we could, but we're going to the Caribbean for the holidays this year," Eliza said. "I'm sorry I can't help."

"Thanks, anyway," Josie said, her shoulders sagging in the billowy reindeer outfit. Clearly she was disappointed, but Oscar wasn't going to be asking anything about it. The last thing he wanted was for Josie to try to rope him into performing. "And I hope you have a great time."

"Thanks," Eliza said. She gave them a small wave and led Jeremy into a patient's room.

As Oscar and Josie walked down the hall, nearly everyone greeted Josie. Oscar couldn't help thinking again how different she was here than at school. Part of it was obviously the costumes—she really stuck out with all the bells and bright colors. But she was also a lot louder around the ward. Maybe here it didn't matter if you were a total weirdo, the way it did at school, so Josie saved it all up for her time volunteering.

Clementine walked beside him, allowing people to pat her or ruffle her ears as they went by. He could really understand why the hospital had started the dog visiting program. Everyone seemed happy to see Clementine.

"Are you coming to visit us today?" a little boy asked, running up to Josie. He looked about five and seemed way too healthy to be in a hospital.

Josie bent down to give him a hug. "Hi, Henry," she said. "We just have one room to visit first and then we'll come see you and Melanie."

"Good," the little boy said, tugging on Josie's antlers. "Everyone's boring and quiet today."

"Well, we'll come by and make some noise to help your sister feel better," Josie said.

So it was his sister, and not Henry, who was sick. That made more sense.

"Come see me, too," Henry said.

"Of course we want to see you, too," Josie said, giving him another quick squeeze.

Henry ran back down the hall, and Josie turned into the room on their left, with Oscar following reluctantly behind. This room, like all the others Oscar had seen so far, had two beds with a curtain between them, a mural on the opposite wall, and a window that looked out onto the parking lot. A toddler was sitting in the first bed, and Josie went right over to her. Oscar stood in the doorway until Josie looked back, then gestured furiously that he should go to the next bed.

Oscar walked as slowly as he could, but it wasn't exactly a long walk. On the other side of the curtain, he saw a girl sitting on the bed, her left leg wrapped up tight and a book in her hands. She looked about seven or eight, and as soon as she saw Clementine, she dropped her book.

"Here, doggy-dog," she called, patting the bed next to her.

"Um, I think maybe you need a sheet or something," Oscar mumbled as Clementine jumped right up on the bed and cuddled in next to the girl.

Oh, well, it wasn't Oscar's fault if she didn't follow the rules. He shifted from one foot to the other, wondering what he was supposed to be doing while the girl hugged Clementine. The room was overheated, and he was getting sweaty in his thick fleece pullover.

"What's the dog's name?" the girl asked.

Oscar cleared his throat. "She's Clementine, and I'm Oscar," he said.

"Like Oscar the Grouch," the girl said cheerfully.

Behind him, Josie burst out laughing. Oscar turned to glare at her. Being called Oscar the Grouch wasn't exactly new or original, and it always irritated him.

But Josie was laughing too hard to notice as she made her way over to them. "Yeah, that's the perfect nickname for Oscar," she told the girl. "And I'm Josie. What's your name?"

"Alison," the girl said.

"Why are you here?" Josie asked.

Oscar had wondered if they were allowed to ask about that, but Josie sounded matter-of-fact, like it was no big deal.

"I tore something in my knee in gymnastics class," Alison said. "I have to have surgery to fix it, and then I'll be coming in for physical therapy. Can I visit Clementine then, too? My mom is allergic to dogs, so we can't get one, but I love playing with them."

As though she understood, Clementine reached up and licked Alison on her chin.

Josie grinned. "You can definitely see her when you come in. She'd love that."

Alison beamed as she scratched Clementine behind the ears. The dog pressed her head against Alison's hand and wagged her short curly tail.

A moment later, a man and woman walked in carrying take-out cartons from Danny's Diner and a bag from Fairy Land Bookstore.

"Mom and Dad, this is Clementine," Alison bubbled. "And Josie and Oscar."

Alison was black while her parents were white, but after considering it Oscar guessed she must have been adopted.

"Nice to meet you," Alison's mom said as her dad set the cartons and books on the table by Alison's bed.

"You too," Josie said. "Do you need me to take the dog out? Alison said you were allergic."

Oscar had already forgotten about that, but Alison's mom just smiled. "Thanks, but I prepared and took my allergy pill," she said. "I want Alison to get her puppy time."

Alison grinned as Clementine snuggled in even closer.

"Want me to sing you some Christmas carols?" Josie asked.

Alison seemed too old for singing, but she surprised Oscar by nodding eagerly. "'O Holy Night' is my favorite. Do you know that one?"

"Yes, and I love it," Josie said. And then she opened her mouth and began to sing. The other day she had only been singing silly songs, so this was the first time Oscar heard her sing for real. And the sound of it stunned him. Her voice soared, rich and sweet, and a hush fell over the room as everyone stopped to take it in.

There was a moment of quiet when she finished, and then Alison, her parents, the parents of the toddler in the next bed, and even some people who had stopped to listen in the hall, burst into applause. Oscar had to admit, at least to himself, that Josie's voice was amazing. And no doubt she would be all full of herself about it now.

But instead her cheeks turned nearly as red as her ridiculous bow, and she waved off the attention. "Now let's sing something together," she told Alison, who agreed as she looked at Josie adoringly.

The two of them sang a few songs, with Alison's parents joining in, too. Then Josie said it was time for them to leave.

"Good luck with your surgery," she told Alison.

"Yeah, good luck," Oscar echoed, glad they were done. He gave Clementine's leash a little tug, and the dog jumped obediently off the bed and followed him out of the room.

"Don't be afraid to ask the kids questions," Josie said as they walked to another room.

Oscar didn't want to ask questions and he certainly didn't appreciate being told what to do. "I know," he said shortly.

Josie glared at him, which just looked absurd with her antlers sticking out like wild antennae. It was kind of hard to believe that someone who looked so outlandish could sing so well.

"How's it going?" Ed asked as he came out of the room beside them.

"Okay," Josie said. "I think we might go see Melanie next."

The elf shook his head. "We stopped by before and her mom said she's not feeling up for any visits besides family today."

Josie sunk down a bit in her costume. "That's rough. Henry's going to be disappointed."

Ed nodded and then headed down the hall.

Josie seemed lost in thought but didn't say anything, and a moment later she led them into a room a few doors down. This one held only one bed, and Oscar could see that it was special, with a bar overhead with some kind of pulley and triangle thing hanging from it. There was a wheelchair next to the bed, and a little girl was propped up on pillows. Her arms were turned up, and Oscar could see that her knees were bent at a sharp angle under the sheet. She broke out into a huge smile when she saw Josie and Clementine.

"Hi, Rosie," Josie said.

"I've been waiting for you," Rosie said, her words slightly slurred but understandable. She looked like she was about five.

"I'm glad to see you," Josie said. "Though I'm sorry you're back in the hospital."

"Actually, it's for a good reason this time," said Rosie's mom, who was sitting on the other side of the bed. "Rosie is getting a hip operation so she can sit more comfortably. It's been known to help a lot of kids who have cerebral palsy like Rosie."

"I might even be able to walk," Rosie said eagerly. Then she looked at Oscar. "Who's he?"

"This is Oscar, like Oscar the Grouch," Josie said cheerfully. "He's going to work in the hospital, too."

"Why is he dressed so boring?" Rosie asked.

"That's a great question," Josie said, her eyes bright as she glanced over at Oscar. "Why don't you ask him?"

Oscar's face was hot and he wanted to snap at Josie, but of course he couldn't, not in front of Rosie. "Ah, I'm like Superman," he said. "Sometimes I have to dress like a normal person, but really it's a disguise." Oscar hoped that would be enough to satisfy Rosie and that Josie would start singing or tap-dancing or whatever.

But Rosie's gaze stayed on Oscar. "Who are you really?" she whispered, like it was top secret information.

Oscar wasn't into make-believe, but the way Rosie looked at him, like he might actually be some kind of superhero, swept Oscar up in the moment. He glanced toward the door, as if checking for anyone listening in, then came closer to the bed so that he could lean down and whisper in Rosie's ear. "Promise you won't tell anyone?"

Rosie nodded, her face solemn.

"I'm Santa's top-secret super spy," he said.

"What do you do?" Rosie whispered. Oscar noticed that her mom was smiling.

"I'm like Santa's number one scout," Oscar said. "Santa sends me out to meet with kids, to decide who gets a lot of gifts, who should get a lump of coal, stuff like that."

"Wow," Rosie said, her voice filled with awe. "What are you going to tell him about me?"

"That you're one of the best kids out there," Oscar told her.

Rosie beamed. Clementine put her paws up on the side of Rosie's bed and yipped, immediately taking Rosie's attention. Rosie's mom and Josie helped settle Clementine on the sheet, leaving Oscar to consider what had happened. He certainly didn't plan to put on a show for all the kids—it was better when Josie did the work and he lurked in the background. But he had to admit it felt good to make Rosie so happy. When Josie started singing a spirited version of "Santa Claus Is Coming to Town," Oscar found himself almost tapping his foot along.

But the second they were out in the hall, Josie spun on her heel and stared him down. "I'm done having you stand around doing nothing while I perform," she told him. "You know how it works now, so you have to start doing something, too."

And just like that every bit of irritation Oscar had felt toward Josie came rushing back, along with the sharp bitterness of his parents' fight that he'd managed to push aside. "Not going to happen." He folded his arms across his chest.

"You have to," Josie insisted.

"Who's going to make me?" Oscar asked tauntingly.

Josie opened her mouth, closed it, then grabbed Clementine's leash and strode down the hall without looking back.

Oscar followed, hating that he had to, hating that he was here instead of at basketball, hating the stupid Christmas carols he could hear one of the elves singing in a room nearby, hating the fact that when this ended he would be stuck going home to his parents who were no doubt still arguing.

In fact, right now Oscar hated just about everything.

Chapter 6

"How'd you do on the math test this morning?" Aisha asked Gabby as they walked toward the cafeteria. Even though they were still around the corner, Gabby could smell the meat loaf. It was a dish she usually enjoyed, but today the smell was making her slightly nauseous.

"Okay, I think," Gabby said, trying to focus on the conversation. There was a heaviness in her body that had been there when she'd woken up, and just walking down the hall felt like work. She must not have slept well because right now all she wanted was to take a nap.

"Hey, guys," Becky said, slightly breathless from having run to catch up to them. "Gabby, are you going to yearbook today?"

"Yes," Gabby said. She didn't enjoy yearbook that much, but she felt it was important to be involved in at least one extracurricular activity. And yearbook was easy.

"Good," Becky said. "It's always more fun when you're there." She rubbed her belly as they neared the cafeteria doors. "I'm starving. I can't wait to get some of that meat loaf."

"Ew, you eat that?" Aisha asked, scrunching up her nose.

"It's good," Becky said defensively.

"I love the meat loaf," Gabby said, slightly distracted by the headache that was beginning to tap at her temples.

"You would," Aisha said with a little laugh. "Hey, are you guys going out for basketball?"

"I don't really have time," Gabby lied. She'd like to play basketball, but she was staying away from sports for reasons she would not be explaining to Aisha or anyone else at school.

"It's a drag how you have to babysit your brothers all the time," Aisha said. "You miss all the good stuff."

Gabby bit back a sharp reply. Luis and Paco were eight-year-old twins, and Gabby loved hanging out with them. They played silly games they made up together, like Zombie Attack and Dragon Tag. For a moment, Gabby imagined what Aisha would think if she could see Gabby in her embroidered jeans and sequined sweaters roaring and flapping her arms dragon-style as she chased both boys down the hall of their small apartment.

"I don't mind," Gabby said as they joined the throng of students heading into the cafeteria. "But you should go out for basketball. I bet it will be really fun."

"I will if you will," Becky said hopefully to Aisha. Aisha shrugged. "Maybe," she said.

"Gabby, Becky, Aisha, wait up," Jasmine called.

Gabby turned and saw Jasmine pushing through the crowd to reach them. Gabby raised her hand to wave, but just then something flickered. At first she thought it was the bright overhead lights with their harsh fluorescent glow. But then she realized the flutter was inside her head, like a bird beating its wings against the side of her skull.

Gabby knew what this meant, and her chest squeezed up so tight, it was hard to breathe.

"I have to go to the girls' room," she managed to say. "I'll see you guys in a minute."

Gabby didn't wait for an answer; she just took off. Once she made it to the bathroom, she locked herself in a stall, sat on the toilet, and let her head fall between her knees. As the blood rushed to her head, the fluttering slowed and then stopped altogether. Gabby waited another moment, then lifted her head slowly and waited. Still no flickering. She stood up. Her legs felt rubbery, like her knees had turned to liquid, but they still held her up. She was okay.

She opened the door of the stall and headed for the sink, stepping gingerly to see if movement would bring back the dreaded light-headed feeling. But nothing happened. She wet a paper towel and pressed its coolness against her cheeks.

Just then, the door opened, and a girl from English, the one who never spoke, Jodi or Josie, walked in. She stopped for a second when she saw Gabby, and then her brows drew together.

"Are you okay?" she asked.

Gabby looked at her reflection in the mirror above the sink and saw that her normally tan cheeks were pasty and her eyes were bloodshot. She looked awful— no wonder the girl was concerned.

"Fine, thanks," Gabby said, not even trying to smile. What bad luck to have someone discover her like this! The girl was just being nice, but Gabby couldn't afford to have anyone wonder about her health, not after what had happened at her old school. She pressed the towel against her cheeks again, hoping to bring some color back into them, but the towel, which was thin, began shredding.

"Do you want to use this?" the girl asked shyly, pulling a folded square of cloth out of her pocket. "I live with my grandparents, and my grandma always makes me carry a handkerchief in the winter."

It was sweet, but Gabby really wished the girl would just leave her alone. "No, thanks," she said.

The girl stuffed the handkerchief back in her pocket and went into a stall.

Gabby pinched her cheeks a few times, which stung, but helped her face look less washed out, then headed into the hall as the warning bell rang. There was no fluttering, nothing to worry about. That was what she told herself as she hurried to the cafeteria.

But her chest and stomach still felt as if something had coiled, snakelike, around them and was squeezing tight. Because she knew what the flickering might mean. And if it was coming back, if her epilepsy was going to reemerge, then her whole life would come crashing down, just like it had the last time.

And Gabby knew she couldn't survive going through that again.

Chapter 7

Monday, December 5

An ambulance siren was howling as Oscar trudged up to the big automatic doors that opened to let him into the hospital. An icy snow fell in wet clumps, and it had soaked through Oscar's wool hat. He pulled it off and stuffed it into his pocket once he was inside the hospital. The smell that greeted him, of lemon cleaner and freshly washed sheets, was starting to be familiar.

The peds ward was the usual bustle of smiling nurses and doctors. There were some new Christmas decorations, including rainbow-colored lights strung down the hall and curled around the desk at the nurse's station. They were obviously meant to be cheery, but the sight of them made Oscar grimace. He was so ready for this stupid holiday to be over so the cold war in his home would thaw, at least a bit, the way it always did after Christmas had passed.

"Hi, Oscar," Ed said cheerfully. Today he was dressed as a reindeer.

"Hey," Jade said. She was wearing a Santa suit and she smiled at Oscar.

Oscar did his best to grin back, but it was hard when they looked so silly. Didn't high school students care about not looking absurd? And didn't they have better things to do with their time?

The two of them headed out, and Oscar sank down on the sofa with a sigh. He wasn't sure if Josie was in the costume closet or just running late, but either way, he planned to treasure every second she wasn't harassing him.

The seconds ended all too soon as Josie flew in a moment later. When she saw Oscar, her face hardened. "You're not coming with me today unless you dress up and sing," she said. "Or help me with a skit. You have to do *something*."

Oscar was about to protest when Clementine, who had come in with Josie, jumped into his lap with a delighted bark.

"Clementine wants me to take her around," Oscar said. That was all the work he was up to today. Clementine butted her wet head against his hand, then looked up at him, her mouth open in a way that made it look like she was smiling. Oscar couldn't help smiling back as he began scratching behind the dog's ears, the way he remembered she enjoyed. Clementine panted happily.

Josie was trying to look skeptical, but clearly the sight of Clementine melted even her Grinch-like heart. "Okay, but this is the last time," she said. "And I mean it."

Oscar was about to disagree when Clementine rolled over, obviously wanting a belly rub. Oscar obliged, petting her cream colored stomach with its thick, downy fur. Clementine wriggled with delight.

Josie hung her puffy coat on the rack, set down her backpack, and disappeared into the costume closet. She reappeared a few minutes later in a bright green elf costume, complete with black boots that had curled toes and a big green elf hat with a bell at the tip. It was all Oscar could do not to snicker. No one was ever going to catch him in something like that, no matter how much Josie threatened.

"First, we'll see if Melanie wants a song," Josie said, leading the way out. As always, everyone said hi as she passed.

Oscar remembered Melanie had been too sick to see them the last time he was there, and he hoped if she was up for a visit that she wasn't contagious.

"Melanie has leukemia," Josie added. "So she has good days and bad."

"That's really awful," Oscar mumbled. He couldn't imagine having an illness that could actually kill you, and the thought made him shiver, despite the heat pumping full blast through the ward.

"Josie, can you come sing to us?" It was Henry, who had come out of room 207 and was grabbing Josie's hand to pull her inside.

"How's your sister?" Josie asked, allowing Henry to lead her.

"Tired like always," Henry said.

"Well, hopefully a song will cheer her up."

But a woman who looked like she hadn't slept or eaten in days came out as they approached the door. "Thanks for coming by, Josie, but Melanie's not up to visitors today."

"I'm sorry to hear it," Josie said, her voice stripped of its usual cheer.

"Sing to *me*," Henry pleaded.

His mother took his hand. "Not now, Henry," she said impatiently. "Josie needs to be with the other sick kids. We'll see her another time."

"When?" Henry whined as his mom dragged him back into the room.

"Hi, Josie and Oscar." Nurse Joe was pushing an empty wheelchair, probably on his way to pick up a patient for a test. "How's it going?"

"Good, and I'm glad we ran into you," Josie said. "I was hoping you and your friends would do your awesome "Night Before Christmas" skit for this year's Christmas Festival."

Oscar took a step back in case anyone had ideas about asking him to participate.

Nurse Joe beamed. "I've been waiting for someone to ask me," he said. "We'd love to—count us in."

"Excellent," Josie said. "Now I just need to find eight more acts."

"You can do it," Nurse Joe said, tucking a stray dreadlock back under his candy cane–printed scrub cap.

"I hope so," Josie said. She was twisting the cuff of her costume, and her forehead was creased. "It seems like everyone is going away for Christmas this year. I don't have that many more people I can ask."

"Some of the cafeteria workers must be around for the holidays," Nurse Joe said. "Otherwise we'd all starve. Remember that awesome big band number they did last year? You should ask them to do it again."

"Right," Josie said. She was looking at a spot on the floor and her voice was muffled, which surprised Oscar. If she cared so much about the show, she should be happy to hear Nurse Joe's suggestions. Not that Oscar planned on pointing that out or anything.

"And those nurses up in infectious disease know how to have fun," Nurse Joe said, starting to push the wheelchair down the hall. "You should ask them, too."

"Good idea," Josie said. She appeared to be trying to smile, but the way the corners of her mouth were stretched, it looked more like she was in pain. Maybe she had a stomachache or something.

"Clementine, come say hi!" a voice called out behind them.

Oscar and Josie turned to see Alison perched up on a pair of crutches, her leg wrapped, reaching a hand out to Clementine.

Oscar led the little dog over, and Alison nearly fell off her crutches in her eagerness to snuggle Clementine close.

"Careful there," Alison's dad said, grabbing her arm before she fell. He looked at Oscar with a smile. "It's so great you guys do this. Instead of worrying about her first physical therapy appointment, Alison's just been talking nonstop about playing with a dog."

"Yeah, it's pretty cool," Oscar said, feeling awkward since he didn't do anything besides lead Clementine around.

"Dad, she's not just a dog. Her name is Clementine," Alison said.

"I stand corrected," her dad said with a grin.

Alison hugged Clementine one last time and then stood up. "Can I see her after I'm done with my appointment?" she asked.

"For sure," Josie said.

Alison and her dad headed down the hall.

"Josie, Freddy's back." A doctor carrying a clipboard had stopped in front of them. She was wearing scrubs printed with holly and a Rudolph pin that had a glowing red nose. "He was asking for you. He's in room 214."

"I'll go see him right now," Josie said. "How is he?"

The doctor frowned. "In a fair amount of pain."

Josie's face clouded, but she nodded and then headed down the hall.

"Should I come, too?" Oscar asked. Someone in a lot of pain sounded kind of tricky, and he hoped Josie would tell him to wait outside.

"Yeah, Freddy likes Clementine," Josie said. Her voice was flat, which sounded all wrong. "He has sickle-cell anemia, by the way."

Oscar wasn't sure what to say since he had no idea what that was.

Josie glanced at him. "It's this disease where your red blood cells are the wrong shape and sometimes they clog up and it really hurts when that happens."

"Can they fix it?" Oscar asked.

A nurse pushing a toddler on a stretcher passed by. The toddler was clutching a stuffed pink rabbit and looked scared, though the nurse was speaking to him in a low, comforting voice.

"Well, the pain will go away eventually, but it can take a while," Josie said. "And it comes back again and again because there's no cure for the disease."

Now Oscar wasn't sure what to say because that seemed really awful and unfair. Just like Melanie's leukemia and seeing a scared toddler were awful and unfair. None of these kids had done anything wrong, and yet all this bad stuff was happening to them. And for the first time Oscar could see why someone might want to dress up and dance and put on silly skits for the patients in the hospital. Not that it took the bad stuff away, but maybe it made them forget, just for a little while, that they were sick.

Still, there was no way *he* was going to do it.

They reached room 214 and headed inside. "Freddy, Josie's here," Freddy's dad said. He was sitting on a chair next to the bed, still in a suit from a day at work. A day that had been interrupted by his son's pain. "And she brought Clementine and a friend to see you." His cheer seemed forced, and Oscar saw that his eyes were bloodshot.

Oscar looked at the boy on the bed, who couldn't have been more than four or five. He was on his side, his knees pulled close to his chest, his brown skin ashen. But he opened his eyes and gave something close to a smile when he saw Josie and her dog. Oscar walked right up to the bed so Freddy could pet Clementine.

"Hey, Freddy," Josie said, brushing the tips of her fingers gently on Freddy's cheek. He seemed to relax the tiniest bit under her touch. Then he reached out a hand to Clementine, who put her paws up on the bed and nuzzled his palm.

Oscar was pretty sure Clementine shouldn't jump all the way up on the bed, not when Freddy was hurting so much, and somehow Clementine must have known that. She stayed where she was, where Freddy could rest his hand on her head.

"Is 'Jingle Bells' still your favorite?" Josie asked Freddy, who nodded, then winced slightly as if even that small movement hurt.

But Josie launched into a merry version of the song, complete with a dance that involved a lot of high stepping with her elf shoes. As Freddy watched, his eyes never leaving Josie, Oscar could see the stiffness seeping out of him, his body sinking into the mattress instead of resting taut on top of it.

Freddy's dad seemed to notice because he smiled and began to clap along with the song.

Josie sang two more carols and then they said good-bye so Freddy could rest. As they walked out, Oscar glanced back at Freddy and noticed his face was just a little softer.

But when Josie spun to face Oscar out in the hall a moment later, her face was the opposite, all sharp edges and narrowed eyes. "That was it," she informed Oscar. "You're done watching me and taking my dog around." She yanked Clementine's leash from him as if to drive the point home. "You can dress up and perform with me or stay in the lounge or whatever. But you're not following me around anymore, not unless you start to pull your weight."

With that, she stalked toward the volunteer room, the bell on her hat ringing violently with every step.

Oscar followed. She could say it as much as she wanted, but he was never going to dress up and perform. And nothing was going to change that. Nothing.

Chapter 8

Monday, December 5

J osie shoved open the door of the volunteer room, then stomped inside. She felt absurd in her elf costume with its dumb bell clinking, and she hated Oscar for it. Because usually there was nothing she loved more than dressing up as an elf and jingling gaily with each step she took. But Oscar's smug glances and hidden snickers had robbed her dress-up and songs of their joy. Which was why she was done with him.

Plus, she had better things to do than escort a burden like Oscar around the hospital: She had to make the Festival happen. And right now it wasn't looking good. Of course, it was great that Ed and Jade and the nurses were signed up. But Josie had already asked most of the other peds volunteers from last year's Festival, and none of them could do it. They would be either away or busy with family coming to town. There was one more person Josie could ask—Charlie had gotten a group of his friends to sing an a cappella medley of carols last year. But aside from him, the other volunteers from last year's Festival worked in different departments so Josie didn't know any of them. And the thought of approaching them made her feel like a swarm of butterflies was trapped in her chest and flapping around furiously.

She pulled off her hat and tossed it on the sofa as Oscar came in. And then she heard the clicking of high heels as Ms. D'Amato walked in behind him. Josie hoped she had some good news about the Festival, but Ms. D'Amato's face was tight and her eyes were darting around the room.

"Have either of you seen Henry?" she asked, without her usual smile or greeting.

Josie's hands clenched into fists at her sides as she thought of Melanie, of how she'd faded from a vibrant redheaded girl to a thin gray shadow. "Is Melanie—?"

"Yes, she's fine," Ms. D'Amato said. "It's Henry. He's missing."

The momentary relief Josie had felt about Melanie fizzled out. Henry was only five, much too young to be wandering around the hospital on his own.

"For how long?" Josie asked, struggling to pull off her elf boots and put on her sneakers so she could help search.

"His parents thought he was in the bathroom," Ms. D'Amato said, pressing her hand to her forehead for a moment. "Melanie was getting a blood draw, so they were distracted, and he must have just slipped out. But that was almost half an hour ago, and no one can seem to track him down."

"I'll help," Josie said.

"That would be great," Ms. D'Amato said. "Oscar, can you tag along with Josie and be an extra set of eyes?"

Josie bit back the no that rose up in her throat and just hoped that Oscar would refuse. But instead he nodded. "Sure."

"Thanks," Ms. D'Amato said, holding the door for them.

After telling Clementine to stay, Josie walked into the hall and headed toward the pediatric lounge with Oscar right behind her. As soon as Ms. D'Amato was out of sight, Josie stopped. "You can just go around by yourself," she told Oscar. She didn't need him wasting her time, not when there was a real emergency.

"I don't know my way around," Oscar said.

"That's not my fault," Josie said, irritated. "You've been following me around for days."

"Just on this one hall," Oscar pointed out.

Josie threw up her arms. "Well, then walk on this one hall," she snapped.

"I'm not going to—"

"Kids, please quiet down." Dr. Scott was standing in front of Freddy's room talking to his dad. At least, she *had* been talking to his dad. Now she was glaring at Josie and Oscar, who were practically yelling right there on the ward.

"Sorry," Josie whispered, tears pricking her eyes. She had never gotten in trouble in the hospital before. This was all Oscar's fault, and he didn't even look the tiniest bit sorry. In fact, he looked like he couldn't care less.

But then he leaned forward, bending down closer to Josie. Oscar was tall, a lot taller than her, but skinny, and he smelled like sneakers and wet wool. "You can't just rush around looking where people have already looked," he said. "You need to try to figure out where you'd want to go if you were in Henry's shoes."

Josie hated to admit it, but that actually made sense.

"That's how they always find missing people on TV," Oscar added.

Josie rolled her eyes. It figured that was Oscar's source of inspiration. But still, it was a good idea. "I think Henry feels left out," Josie said, remembering Henry begging them to perform for him and not just Melanie. "And maybe angry at his parents."

"No, not like that," Oscar said impatiently. "It's like if he loves candy, you go to the candy machine."

"That's stupid," Josie said. Why did Oscar have to be so endlessly maddening? "And all kids like candy, so that's not exactly a revelation."

"Well, did anyone look for him at the vending machines?" Oscar asked, his voice getting louder.

Josie was about to say that it would be a waste of time when every second counted. But then she realized it might actually be worth a look. "Fine," she said between clenched teeth, leading them through the doors of the ward to the main hall, where there was a small alcove of vending machines near the restrooms. An alcove that was empty.

"See?" Josie said smugly.

"Well, there're probably other places to get food," Oscar said in a crabby voice. "Plus, maybe Henry isn't as big into candy. Maybe he likes video games."

"There's no arcade at the hospital," Josie snapped. "Plus, Henry isn't into video games. He likes singing and . . ." Josie's voice trailed off, her heart starting to thump just a little harder. Henry liked singing and the shows they performed. That was what he had been asking for. And it was most likely what he had gone to find.

"I think I know where he is," Josie said. She spun around and hurried back to the volunteer room, Oscar following.

Clementine was not there, which normally would have worried Josie but instead confirmed her hunch. And sure enough, when they walked into the closet crowded with racks of costumes and shelves of shoes, they saw Henry sitting in the corner, Clementine curled next to him.

"Henry, everyone's worried about you," Josie exclaimed, stumbling over a pair of black buckled boots as she rushed over to him.

"No, they're not," Henry said. His eyes were red-rimmed and his chin trembled. "They're only worried about Melanie."

Josie knew they needed to tell his parents and everyone else that Henry was okay, but she couldn't just walk out, not when he was so upset and clearly needed to talk. So she sat down on the floor next to Henry and was surprised when Oscar did the same.

"Your parents love you," Josie said, reaching for the little boy's hand. "But I know they spend a lot of time talking about your sister."

"All the time, always," Henry said. His eyes brimmed with tears.

Josie got that. She didn't want to say so in front of Oscar, but she had no choice. She looked right at Henry and tried to forget Oscar was there.

"I know how that feels," she said. "When my dad was sick, my mom practically lived in the hospital."

Henry looked her in the eyes for the first time since they'd found him in the closet, so Josie knew she needed to go on.

"It was like she forgot she was a mom, and that was hard," Josie said. "Really hard."

"What did you do?" Henry asked.

Josie smiled sadly. "What you do," she said. "I talked to the people in the hospital. They were really good at taking care of me and making me feel better. And then my grandparents came, and that helped, too. I missed my mom, but later she was ready to be a mom again." Josie hoped Henry would not ask how long it had taken. Things had been pretty rough after her dad died and that was why she and her mom had needed to move in with her grandparents. But it had gotten better, and it would for Henry, too. And hopefully his story would also include Melanie healing.

Henry rested his hands on Clementine's back,

pushing his fingers into her thick fur. "Did your mom yell, too?"

"Um, what do you mean?" Josie asked, not sure where Henry was going with this.

"When we get home, my mom and dad yell about Melanie," Henry said, looking only at Clementine.

Josie wasn't sure what to say to that. It made sense that with all the stress Henry's parents would sometimes argue. But she hated how Henry was once again blinking back tears.

"My parents argue a lot, too."

Josie nearly fell over. It was Oscar speaking, and he was gazing steadily at Henry.

Henry looked up at Oscar. "Does it scare you?" he asked softly.

Oscar paused, then nodded. "Yeah, it scares me."

Josie knew she was pretty much gaping, but she couldn't stop herself. It was as though Oscar had been taken over by an alien. A kind, compassionate alien who was opening up so that Henry would not feel alone.

And it was working. Henry scrunched over so that he was leaning against Oscar. Oscar tensed for a moment and then gently put his arm around the little boy.

Then Oscar looked at Josie, and she knew in that moment that everything had changed.

Chapter 9

Tuesday, December 6

"Nice job, Gabby," Ms. Robinson said as she handed Gabby her math test back. She had just finished telling the class that over half of them had failed, so the big red A on top was especially pleasing.

"Thanks," Gabby said. And then she felt it, the tiniest flutter of wings at the back of her skull. "Um, I need to run to the girls' room."

"Sure," Ms. Robinson said, her brow wrinkling slightly. Gabby realized she had probably sounded desperate.

But there was no time to worry about that now, and in truth, Gabby *was* desperate. The wings were beating faster, her hands were starting to feel numb, and Gabby knew what that meant. She nearly ran out of the room and down the hall, pushing open the bathroom door and sinking to her knees before the light came, harsh and white. And then everything went blank.

THERE WAS BLOOD on her face. It was the first thing she realized when she came to. Luckily, she'd been sitting down, so she probably hadn't gotten a concussion, something that had happened once at her old school. But after feeling for the source of the sticky, warm wetness she realized that she'd fallen hard enough to split open her eyebrow. It was just a little cut, but one that was bleeding. A lot. Plus, her head was pounding like someone had hit it with a large hammer while she lay unconscious on the floor for who knew how long.

For a moment Gabby considered standing up, cleaning off her face, and going back to class like nothing had happened. But her head hurt, the blood scared her, and with sickening certainty, Gabby realized that this was happening and she couldn't hide from it. And so when she was able, she got slowly to her feet, washed off her face, and then walked carefully down the hall to the main office.

"I need to call my dad," Gabby said to the secretary, who seemed ready to protest until she took a good look at Gabby.

"Sure, hon, and why don't you sit while you call," the secretary said kindly, gesturing to a chair as she pushed the phone toward Gabby.

"Thanks," Gabby said, and meant it. Her shaky legs were not doing a great job holding her up. She dialed the number for her dad and then waited while someone paged him to come in from the factory floor. She hated to take her dad away from work, but it was harder for her mom to leave in the middle of the day, so there wasn't much choice.

"Gabs, what's wrong?" her father asked breathlessly. Gabby knew he had run all the way to the factory office, and she had to blink back tears.

"I'm sick," she said. "Can you come?"

"I'm on my way," her dad said, his voice strong.

"DON'T BE SCARED, *mi hija*," her father said a half hour later as they drove to Frost Ridge County Hospital. "Dr. Klein just wants us to go to the hospital so she can run some tests, see what's going on. She probably missed something small at your appointment last week. It will be fine." His musical voice usually comforted Gabby, but not today.

"Okay," she whispered, staring down at her hands clenched in her lap.

They were stopped at a red light, and her dad rubbed her shoulder. "Dr. Klein said this might happen," he reminded her. "As you grow up, the medication will need some adjustments."

"Okay," Gabby said again. She knew her dad was trying to help, but he would never understand what really scared her. She was pretty sure the doctor would be able to help, and after some trial and error, the new medication would work pretty well. But it was the trial and error that was the problem because it left her vulnerable to having a seizure at school. And that was the scariest possibility of all.

There were probably plenty of girls in plenty of places who had epilepsy, and it was no big deal. But Gabby had not been one of those girls. Her first-ever seizure had happened when she was over at her best friend Jenny's house. She'd felt the numbness, the nausea, that moment of light, and then everything went blank. When she'd come to, Jenny had been standing over her, her eyes wide.

"I thought you were dead," Jenny said.

"Yeah, me too," Gabby said, her heart still thumping crazily in her chest. "But I think I'm okay." She struggled to sit up, and that was when she realized that her embroidered jeans and the spot on the white rug where she lay were soaked.

"Oh," Jenny said, stepping back. "Um, I'll get you a towel." The words were kind, but her voice was pinched, and Gabby saw the way her whole face scrunched up. It was obvious she thought Gabby was disgusting. And sitting there on the carpet in a puddle of her own urine, Gabby had felt the exact same way.

Jenny had only told a few people about the incident, but gossip like that traveled fast. In just half a day, Gabby had been given the nickname Bed Wetter, which didn't make sense but apparently Rug Wetter wasn't as good a name. After Gabby was diagnosed, she tried telling people, but a group of boys had dubbed epilepsy the "pee disease," so it made everything even worse. Gabby had always known Jenny had trouble keeping secrets, but she'd never imagined Jenny would spill one about her. Especially one so damaging. Jenny called to apologize, but soon after that, she stopped returning Gabby's texts, averting her eyes whenever they passed in the hall at school, as though they had never been friends at all. Gabby had spent the final weeks of fourth grade a total outcast, the girl who no one looked at but everybody snickered about when she walked down the halls alone.

Her family's move had been a chance to start over, to be a regular girl who didn't have a gross, humiliating illness. Because at this point, just hearing the word *epilepsy* made Gabby's skin all hot and itchy, like she'd broken out in oozing hives. The disease had ruined her life once, but as long as no one at Frost Ridge Middle School found out about it, that wouldn't happen again. And so Gabby had done—and would continue to do—everything she could to make sure no one ever came close to discovering the truth.

Dr. Klein met them at the hospital entrance with a wheelchair for Gabby, which she knew was standard hospital protocol. It was a relief to sink into the chair and allow herself to be pushed to where she needed to go. Her head still pounded and walking hurt.

It took about three hours to run through the first battery of tests, and at the end, Gabby was sent up to the pediatric ward, where she'd stay for the next few days.

"It's a nice hospital," her dad said as he straightened the curtain between her bed and the empty one beside it.

"Yeah," Gabby agreed absently. This was her first time at the Frost Ridge hospital, and the doctors, nurses, and lab technicians had taken the time to explain things to her, which she appreciated. But a hospital was a hospital, and she was already counting the hours until she could leave.

"Luis will like the mural," her dad said as he stood next to her bed and gestured to the colorful paintings of knights in battle. It was just the kind of thing artistic Luis enjoyed drawing.

"Paco too," Gabby said. "He likes anything with swords."

"That he does," her father agreed, ruffling her hair gently. Although her head still ached, it felt good, both comforting and familiar. "I need to go pick up the boys, but we'll be back in a few minutes. And I know your mom will be here the second she can leave work."

"Okay," Gabby said, hoping he would hurry. It was kind of babyish, but it felt better to have her dad close.

She glanced at the clock and realized she was missing yearbook—Becky would have a lot to say about that. Gabby would need a good explanation for leaving in the middle of the day. The flu maybe? Or had she used that excuse recently? It was too much to figure out now, so she took a sip of water, then leaned back against the pillows and picked up the remote for the TV.

Dr. Klein came in a few minutes later, a nurse on her heels. "Are you settling in okay?" she asked Gabby, resting a hand on Gabby's knee.

"Yes, thanks," Gabby said. She clicked off the TV, since there wasn't anything good on local cable, which was the only channel that was working.

"I'm going to leave you with Nurse Joe," Dr. Klein said, and the nurse in a Santa hat and reindeer-printed scrubs smiled at Gabby. "He'll let you know about life on the ward."

"It's like a dungeon up here," the nurse said, then threw out his arms. "I'm just kidding! We have a great time."

Gabby smiled feebly as there was obviously no such thing as a great time in a hospital. Though at least here she was safe from anyone at school finding out her secret.

"We'll get you a menu so you can choose your meal options," Nurse Joe said. "And every afternoon we have a craft or activity in the lounge. Today they're making Christmas tree decorations."

"Um, I'm kind of tired," Gabby said. "I think I might just want to stay in bed." She was in no mood to do an art project.

"Sure, but don't worry," Nurse Joe said, assuming she was disappointed to miss out. "There are other things you can do right here in your room. We have volunteers who will come sing for you. There's also a canine visitation program, where owners bring in carefully screened dogs to spend time with patients. Your doctor said you're cleared for a visit if you want one, so I can see if any of them are around now."

At that, Gabby nodded. She had always loved animals, especially dogs.

"Okay, then," Nurse Joe said. "I'll let you rest now. Just ring the buzzer if you need anything."

"Thanks," Gabby said as Nurse Joe walked out. He pushed through the door, but after he left, it only closed about halfway before coming to a stop. "Hmm, this must be a little jammed," he said, poking his head back in. "I'll have someone come look at it."

"Thanks," Gabby said again. She definitely wanted a door that closed.

Nurse Joe pushed the door closed behind him, and Gabby lay back on her bed with a sigh. This was bad, but it would be okay. Dr. Klein would regulate her medication, and in a few days, she'd be back at school, ready with a story about a killer cold or a stomach bug that had knocked her out. The seizures would stop, no one would find out where she'd really been, and Gabby's life would go back to normal.

Just then, two people passed her door, kids her

age. For a fleeting second, she thought the boy looked familiar, but then they were gone, and Gabby figured she'd just imagined it.

There was no way anyone from school would be here in the hospital, she was sure of it.

Chapter 10

❦

Wednesday, December 7

"You don't want to be the Grinch? He's my favorite," Josie said, coming out of the costume closet in a plush reindeer costume that Oscar had seen her wear before. The final touch was the red rubber nose she wore, Rudolph-style. "Or maybe just wear a Santa hat?" The nose made her voice slightly nasal.

Oscar, who was on the sofa in the volunteer room with Clementine snug on his lap, shook his head. "Nope," he said. He'd agreed to sing and that was as far as it was going.

"But it's so much more fun to perform in costumes," Josie said, sitting down next to him with a loud jingle. "And the kids really love it."

Clementine reached out to lick her owner's hand, and Josie rubbed the dog's head. Clementine did her usual wriggle to position Josie's hand near her ears, her favorite scratching spot, which made Oscar smile. Clementine knew how to get what she wanted.

"Isn't it enough that I'll sing?" Oscar asked.

"Yeah, but I don't get why you won't even wear one little elf hat, too," Josie said. Now she was rubbing Clementine under her chin, which the dog clearly loved as well. Clementine closed her eyes and gave a little sigh of contentment.

"I'm just not into Christmas," Oscar said with a shrug, like it was no big deal.

"What?!" Josie gasped like he'd announced a plan to abolish gift giving or outlaw candy.

Clementine's eyes snapped open at the sharp sound, and Oscar reached over and patted her soft back. Normally, he wouldn't say any more, but Josie already knew about his parents fighting so it didn't seem like that big a deal to tell her why. Plus she was easy to talk to. "It's just, my parents argue more around the holidays," Oscar said.

As though sensing that this was hard, Clementine moved closer to him and reached up to give him a lick on the cheek. Oscar patted her gently on the back and wondered why he had never realized how awesome dogs were. Especially this one.

"Oh," Josie said, sitting back. "Yeah, that makes sense. I know my mom loves Christmas, but it kind of stresses her out, too."

"Exactly," Oscar said. "And when they're stressed, they fight about everything, twenty-four seven."

"That is rough," Josie said with a sigh, like she knew exactly what he was talking about.

And Oscar felt the littlest bit better having told her. But it wasn't going to change the costume situation.

"So, yeah, since I'm anti-Christmas, I'm not wearing a costume," he said.

"But you'll sing carols?" Josie asked, a note of anxiety in her voice. "I mean, we sing Hanukkah songs for some kids, but most of them really want Christmas songs this time of year."

"I know," Oscar said. He'd resigned himself to that. "But that's as far as I go."

"Okay," Josie said, standing up. "I get it."

She really did, and Oscar couldn't help being grateful.

Oscar shifted gently, and Clementine hopped off his lap, ready to go. But instead of heading for the door, Josie disappeared back in the costume room.

"You can wear these," she told him a moment later, handing him a Yankees baseball cap and a pair of oversized sunglasses.

"Um, why?" he asked, his brows scrunching together.

"It's a costume," Josie explained, setting the cap on his head. "Remember how you told Rosie you were Santa's spy or superhero or whatever?" she said. "You'll be the spy of Christmas."

At that, Oscar shook his head. "How about the Superhero Super Agent?"

Josie winced. "Um, what about Santa's Secret Agent?"

Oscar considered, then nodded.

"Awesome," Josie crowed. She took a pair of felt antlers out of the folds of her costume and positioned them on Clementine's head, transforming the small dog into a miniature reindeer. Clementine seemed fine with this, pausing to sniff the table for any tasty crumbs and then giving herself a shake, as though readying for the work ahead. "Let's go perform."

That was when Oscar realized his pulse was skittering and his mouth felt like he'd just chewed up a big ball of cotton. He wasn't much of a singer. What if people laughed at him?

"It's easier in a costume," Josie said, like she'd just read his mind.

When he looked at her, he saw that she was pulling at a lock of hair. "People always ask me why I'm shy everywhere but here on the peds ward," she said. "And part of it is the kids and how it's not a big deal to sing for just a few of them and they're so happy and stuff. But the other part is the costumes. It's like you're kind of hiding when you wear one."

That made a lot of sense. Oscar pulled the cap down and slipped on the sunglasses. His mouth was still dry, but it did feel safer behind the dark glasses and hat. "Let's do this," he said.

Josie gave him a thumbs-up, passed Oscar Clementine's leash, and led the way into the hall. Thankful to have the dog with him, Oscar took a deep breath and followed.

"Looking good, Oscar," a doctor called as he passed. Oscar hadn't realized any of the staff knew who he was.

"Thanks," he said, grinning. The colored lights strung along the hall were blinking, covering them in splashes of red, gold, and green as they walked. The Christmas tree at the nurse's station glittered with tinsel and bright ornaments, and they passed a room where a family was laughing together over a story a little boy was telling. This hospital had its share of bad things, but Oscar was starting to see that it could be a happy place, too, at least in some ways.

One of the nurses was pushing an empty wheel-chair, and she cheered when she saw Oscar. "I knew our girl Josie would get you dressed up," she said. "You go, Oscar."

Oscar had to laugh at that.

"See, costumes are fun," Josie said.

Oscar had to admit that they kind of were, at least cool ones like his.

Freddy was clearly not in as much pain today. When they walked into his room, they found him sitting up, his brown cheeks glowing. Clementine jumped right on his bed, making Freddy grin.

"Whoa, you're a spy!" Freddy shouted when he saw Oscar.

Oscar grinned and reached out to give Freddy a high five. "I'm Santa's Secret Agent," he said.

Freddy's eyes widened. "That's awesome," he said. "Do you go on missions?"

Oscar nodded solemnly. "All the time," he said as seriously as he could.

Freddy was looking at Oscar like he really was a secret agent, and a superhero, too. This whole costume thing really was okay. If only he didn't have to sing.

"Ready?" Josie asked Oscar quietly.

Oscar gulped, then nodded.

And so they began.

Oscar messed up some of the words to "Jingle Bells," and he didn't know all the verses for "Deck the Halls," but it didn't matter. Freddy shrieked and clapped the whole time, and his mom, who still had dark circles under her eyes, smiled and cheered. It kind of made Oscar feel like a rock star. A rock star who sang carols, but still.

"You loved it," Josie said when they were done and on their way to see Rosie. It wasn't a question.

"It's not so bad," Oscar admitted. He *had* loved it, though he wasn't quite ready to admit it.

Josie smirked. "Right, it was just okay."

"Hey, Oscar, you're going undercover," Ed called as he and Jade passed dressed as Christmas trees. "I like it."

"Looking good," Jade agreed, giving him a thumbs-up with her green-gloved hand.

"You're a hit," Josie said, smiling as they came up to the nurse's station.

"A snickerdoodle for Santa's Secret Agent," Nurse Joe said, passing Oscar a tray.

"How'd you know what my costume was?" Oscar asked, carefully selecting a cookie that looked extra crusted with cinnamon and sugar. He took a big bite, the thick, buttery cookie melting in his mouth, the sugar and cinnamon sweet on his tongue.

Nurse Joe winked. "Word travels fast here on the ward," he said. "It's kind of like the Wild West, only we battle illness instead of outlaws."

Oscar did his best not to roll his eyes at how cheesy Nurse Joe was, but he did thank him for the cookie that he wolfed down in three bites.

"He's goofy, but the kids love him," Josie said as Nurse Joe headed down the hall. She popped her last bite of cookie in her mouth, licked the sugar off her lips, and brushed a few cookie crumbs off her hands.

Oscar guessed that there were worse things than being cheesy, especially when you worked with little kids. Not that he planned to be talking about the Wild West anytime soon.

Just then, Clementine gave a short bark and began wagging her curlicue of a tail so hard her hindquarters swayed. Coming toward them was a man walking a shaggy black-and-white dog who barked back in happy greeting.

"Hey, Charlie," Josie said as the two dogs began to sniff each other enthusiastically. "This is Oscar, otherwise known as Santa's Secret Agent."

"I like it," Charlie said with a grin. "I'm guessing you get trusted with some pretty high-level jobs for the old man up north."

Oscar laughed. "Yep, all the time."

"Charlie, I was hoping we'd see you," Josie said. "Can you and your friends perform in the Christmas Festival again this year?"

"I wish I could, but we have family coming to town," he said, sounding genuinely disappointed. "I'm going to be real busy the week leading up to the holiday."

"No big deal," Josie said. She was slumped down in her costume, and Oscar could see that it was clearly a *very* big deal. He remembered her talking to Nurse Joe about it a few days ago and realized he'd better change the subject fast or she'd think to ask him to help out. And while Oscar might be up to singing to a patient or two, there was no way he was singing in front of an audience.

"Let's go see Rosie," he said, leading the way to her room.

Rosie had a cast around her hips where she'd had surgery, but her face lit up when she saw them. "Mama, it's Santa's Secret Agent!" she cried.

"At your service," Oscar said with a grin.

Chapter 11

Wednesday, December 7

"Gabby, Gabby," her brothers squealed as they barreled into her room and jumped onto her bed.

"*Niños,*" Gabby's father scolded, but Gabby was laughing.

"It's okay," she said, wrapping one arm around Luis while Paco bounced happily at the end of the bed. He could never stay still for very long.

"How was school?" she asked her brothers.

"Boring," Paco said, wrinkling his nose.

Gabby usually told him how important it was to study, but today she just felt sympathetic. "The hospital is boring, too," she told him.

"No one came to play with you?" Luis asked, his brow creasing.

"Not one person came to play," Gabby said in mock sadness. Her brothers always brought out her silly side. "But someone did come to take my blood."

Her brothers shrieked in delight as she'd known they would.

"A vampire?" Paco asked, leaning forward.

Gabby made her eyes wide, like she did at home when they played Dragon Tag. "I think so," she whispered, glancing behind her like she was worried a vampire might leap out. "She had really sharp teeth."

"We need a stake and some garlic," Paco announced. "I can't believe we left the monster weapon box at home."

"We'll have to make a new one," Gabby said, feeling better than she had in days. "There's a toothbrush in the bathroom that would make a great stake."

Paco raced off for the toothbrush while Luis slipped more slowly off the bed. Gabby lost track of him as Paco returned and began running around the room to show them how he'd tackle a vampire if one arrived.

Gabby was about to ask if this technique would work on zombies as well, because they all knew that wherever there were vampires, there were always a few zombies. But then the door opened, and Nurse Joe came in, followed by Luis and two other people. When Gabby realized who they were, she sat up with a gasp, her whole body rigid as adrenaline coursed through her. This couldn't be happening.

"I brought friends for you," Luis said proudly, gesturing to the quiet girl from Gabby's English class and Oscar Madison, the boy who'd recently been suspended for fighting. The girl was wearing an elaborate getup involving yards of red and green satin, a ton of bells, and a big Santa hat while Oscar wore a baseball hat and sunglasses and was petting the fluffy tan dog that was with them. The dog snuggled against him for a moment but then came over to sniff Gabby's hand, its tightly curled tail wagging.

Normally, Gabby loved dogs, but right now she was frozen in horror, unable to move or even think. How was it possible that two kids from school were here, in her hospital room, on the verge of finding out the thing that would destroy Gabby's life?

"These are some of our hospital volunteers who I told you about yesterday," Nurse Joe said, happily oblivious to Gabby's dismay. "They'll sing or maybe do a short skit for you while you play with Clementine here." Nurse Joe bent down and gave the dog a vigorous rub on her back. The dog rewarded him with a lick on his cheek.

"Careful, they might be vampires," Paco whispered, brandishing the toothbrush.

Gabby wished they were vampires. That would be a million times better than what was actually happening.

"Hello," Gabby's dad said, standing up to greet the two volunteers.

"Hi, I'm Josie, and this is Oscar," Josie said, smiling at him. "We're happy to meet all of you. And we're in Gabby's class at school." She hadn't actually looked at Gabby once since coming into the room.

"Wonderful," Gabby's father said, clearly thinking this was a great coincidence instead of a complete disaster.

Paco marched up to them. "A vampire came and took my sister's blood," he announced. "So you need to be really careful around here."

Why wouldn't her brother stop talking? And how could she get Oscar and the girl out of here? Sweat prickled on her palms, and Gabby took a deep breath, trying to think of a way to end this.

Josie laughed. "The vampires here help people get better," she said. "They'll have your sister fixed up in no time."

"Actually, she—" Paco began, obviously about to spill everything. And that finally spurred Gabby to action. She put up a hand and coughed.

"Thanks for coming by," she said, a little too loudly. "But I'm really tired and I'm sure you have lots of other kids to see, so I don't think I need a show today."

"But I want to see them sing." Paco moaned like Gabby had just suggested he give up his entire LEGO collection.

"Paco, maybe we can watch them sing in another room," Gabby's dad said. "We don't want to disturb your sister."

"Sure, come with us," Josie said.

This wasn't good, either. But Paco was talking about Christmas carols and Luis was asking Oscar if he could try on the sunglasses, so it seemed like the danger of them telling Gabby's secret had passed, at least for the moment.

Gabby sat back as the group of them pushed through the door of her room out into the hall. The door closed halfway and then stopped. Nurse Joe hadn't gotten anyone to come look at it yet.

She sighed. She didn't want to be lying here with the door partly open so that anyone could look in. Who knew if anyone else from the sixth grade might walk by? Now that she'd seen Oscar and Josie, it seemed possible that her entire class could be here. She stood up to go push the door shut, and a sharp pain zipped from behind her left eye through to the back of her skull. She paused and then it was gone. She started for the door again and the pain came back, this time with a blinding flash. And then there was nothing.

* * * ✦ * * *

GABBY WAS AWARE of something soft under her. Something soft that was licking her hand. Her eyes flew open, and she saw that she'd fallen, but somehow the dog, Clementine, was under her. It seemed like she had gotten there fast enough to break Gabby's fall because nothing on her body was hurting.

"Are you okay?"

"What happened?"

Gabby looked up. There in the doorway stood Oscar and Josie, their eyes wide as they looked at Gabby in a crumpled heap. Gabby pressed at the floor and her hospital gown frantically, but both were dry. So at least the very worst thing hadn't happened. But this was still a disaster. Her head was pounding and her body was shaky and weak.

"I—" Gabby began, but her father and Nurse Joe were rushing in.

"Gabby, you had a seizure," Nurse Joe said,

crouching down next to her while Gabby's father eased his arm carefully around Gabby.

"Clementine jerked her leash out of my hand and ran in," Josie said, like she couldn't believe what had just happened. "I've heard that dogs can sense seizures, and I guess it's true. She got to you just when you fell and she stood under you so you wouldn't hit your head or anything."

At this point, Gabby kind of wished she had hit her head and been knocked out cold so that Oscar and Josie would have to leave.

"Don't worry," Nurse Joe said, putting an arm around Gabby so he and her dad could help her back to the bed. "It's normal for there to be some glitches as we work on getting your meds balanced."

"Right," Gabby said. It hurt to talk, but she needed to say something, anything to make Josie and Oscar leave before someone said the dreaded word that would seal Gabby's doom. "And I—"

"We'll call Dr. Klein, let her know what happened," Nurse Joe went on. "But I've seen a lot of kids with epilepsy, and this happens, so don't be scared. We'll get you sorted and have you out of here in no time."

Gabby stopped listening because nothing he said mattered now. The only things that mattered were the way Josie's mouth fell open and she grabbed Oscar's arm. And the way Oscar's lip curled up. They were both disgusted. It was obvious. And it was just a question of time before they told everyone at school.

And then Gabby's life would be over again.

Chapter 12

🌿

Sunday, December 11

"Ready for pancakes?" Josie's mom asked, sticking her head into Josie's room. Every Sunday morning, Josie and her mom went to Danny's Diner for brunch.

"Yeah, I just have to brush my hair," Josie said. She was already dressed in a pair of green corduroys and the bright red reindeer sweater her grandmother had knit for her this year. She wouldn't dress like this for school, but on weekends, especially when she was going to Danny's with her mom, she liked getting festive.

Her room was pretty festive, too. Her sky-blue walls were normally decorated with animal posters, but every Christmas she pulled out the prints her grandmother had ordered for her: pictures of Christmas scenes by famous artists and a poster from *Elf,* her favorite Christmas movie. On her dresser were photos of family Christmases past, little Josie on her dad's lap while her mom helped her open presents, then later years with her grandparents by the tree they decorated with homemade ornaments. Strings of white Christmas lights hung from the ceiling, completing her holiday theme.

"Want me to do a French braid?" her mom asked, coming into her room.

Josie grinned and nodded. Her mom was a French-braiding master, plus Josie loved when her mom brushed her hair. It made her scalp all tingly.

Her mom stood behind her, and Josie closed her eyes as her mom gently pulled the brush through Josie's hair.

"How's school?" her mom asked.

"Everything's good," Josie said, opening her eyes and looking at her mom's reflection in the mirror. "I got a ninety-five on my last math test, and Ms. Keller liked my essay on *The Outsiders* in English."

"Nice," her mom said with a nod, her eyes focused as she began dividing Josie's hair into sections. "And how are things at the hospital?"

"Good," she said, thinking of Oscar, Santa's Secret Agent. "Great, even."

"And the Festival?" her mom asked. "It's getting close to the big day."

Ever since Charlie had said no, Josie had vowed she'd start asking non–peds ward volunteers to sign up. She'd even walked part way into the OB-GYN ward to ask one of the doctors there. But her heart began thumping, her face boiled, and she worried she might be having a heart attack right there in the hall. So she'd headed back to safety and made a sign, which she'd posted on the staff bulletin board. It had seemed like a good idea, but so far no one had responded. "I have two acts set," she said. "And nine days to find eight more." Saying it out loud made Josie's stomach twist up like it was her insides being braided.

"What have you done to get volunteers?" her mom asked. She was weaving the locks of hair snugly, pulling on Josie's scalp and making her wince slightly. But Josie knew the braid had to be tight or it would start coming loose in less than an hour.

"I asked some people who performed in the show last year," Josie said, tugging at a stray piece of yarn on the cuff of her sweater. "And I put up a sign."

"Maybe you could get a list of people who performed in the past three or four years," her mom suggested. "I bet there were people last year who couldn't do it but would like to now."

"That's a great idea," Josie said, letting go of her sleeve as she thought about it. There was a good chance some of the peds staff had been away last year but performed in years past. In fact, she vaguely remembered Dr. Scott playing the saxophone one year. She'd email Ms. D'Amato for the lists as soon as they were home from Danny's. And maybe she'd get away with not having to approach the non–peds staff at all.

Her mom fastened the braid and then raised one eyebrow as she looked at Josie. "It's good practice to talk to people like this," she said, reading Josie's mind like she often did. "Speaking up for yourself is an important life skill."

Josie's mom was big on life skills, all of which seemed to involve something unpleasant. Which Josie was about to point out when her stomach growled loudly. Josie pressed her hands against her middle as her mom laughed, which made Josie break into giggles. Her mom had the best laugh, like the clinking of the delicate glass ornaments on their Christmas tree—mixed with occasional goose honks.

"Sounds like we better get to Danny's," her mom said, leading the way downstairs.

The two of them piled on jackets, scarves, and hats and headed out into the bright frigid morning. The wind blew little ice crystals that stung Josie's cheeks as they walked, but the sun shining on the snow made it glitter like jewels were hidden just beneath the surface.

A few minutes later, they walked into the bustling warmth of Danny's Diner, where Maggie, their usual server, seated them in their usual booth along the back wall. Christmas carols played softly in the background, tinsel and paper rings hung from the walls, and the little tree next to the register added the scent of pine to the Saturday morning smells of coffee and pancakes fresh off the griddle.

"Two stacks of blueberry cornmeal pancakes, right?" Maggie asked as she poured Josie's mom a cup of decaf.

"Yes, thanks," Josie's mom said with a smile.

"So what's the best thing that happened this week?" Josie's mom asked once they had ordered. This was how they always started their brunches, but today Josie noticed that her mom was blinking a lot and her hands played absently with an empty sugar packet. She hadn't seemed distracted at home, but now it looked like there was something on her mind. Sometimes when she had news, she waited to tell Josie over their meal. Josie just hoped today's news was good, like a spring break trip to Disney World.

"The best thing this week is that Oscar's singing with me now," Josie said. She'd already told her mom the whole story in detail, and it was definitely the best part of the week.

"Right, that's pretty awesome," her mom said, now folding the packet into a small square.

"What about you?" Josie asked. Usually her mom didn't need prompting to finish their ritual.

"Oh, I think it was when the carolers stopped by the post office right before closing on Friday," her mom said, smiling at the memory.

"Did they sing 'Angels We Have Heard on High'?" Josie asked. It was her mom's favorite.

Her mom nodded. "Yes, though not as beautifully as you sing it," she said. "You should really perform it for the Festival."

Josie was certainly not interested in having this conversation again. She was about to get things back on track and ask more about the carolers when she heard someone shout her name. She turned to see Henry running toward her, nearly banging into Maggie, who just grinned at his exuberance.

"Hi, Henry," Josie said as he crawled up next to her for a hug. He had a ring of hot chocolate around his mouth and smelled sweet, like syrup. "This is my mom."

Henry's eyes got wide. "You have a mom?" he asked.

Josie's mom laughed. "She sure does."

"You're the nice lady at the post office," Henry said, clearly confused that Josie's mom might have more than one role in his life.

"That's my day job," Josie's mom said. "At night, I'm a mom."

"Just like Dad and I run the dry cleaners, but we take care of you and Melanie, too," Henry's mom said, coming up to their table.

Henry's forehead was still creased, as though it was all too much to take in, but then he grinned at Josie. "My mom took me out for waffles," he said. "Just me."

Josie grinned back. "That's pretty special," she said. She decided she'd text Oscar about it.

"It is," Henry's mom said with a smile. She reached for Henry's hand, and the two of them headed out.

"Here we go," Maggie said, setting steaming stacks of pancakes down in front of Josie and her mom.

Danny's blueberry cornmeal pancakes were famous throughout Frost Ridge, and Josie and her mom focused as they spread them with butter and poured on maple syrup from the farm outside town.

Josie took her first bite, the sweet syrup mixing with the tart blueberry, and waited for her mom to tell her what was going on. It was probably something small, like a change in her shift schedule for the holidays. But a whisp of worry brushed icily along the back of her neck.

"There's something I wanted to talk to you about," her mom said finally, reaching for another sugar packet. "I think it's time for you and me to find a place of our own."

This was not what Josie had expected. "Why?" she asked. Everything was fine right where they were.

"Well, after Dad died, I needed your grandparents," her mom said. "We both did."

Josie nodded.

"But it's been five years," her mom went on. "And I think it's time for me to move on, to be your mom full-time and, you know, be a grown-up."

Josie grinned at her mom's joke, but inside she was reeling. Living with her grandparents in their cozy house was perfect. Moving out on their own sounded risky, and Josie was not a fan of risks.

"You can be a grown-up at Grandma and Grandpa's house," Josie said, swirling a chunk of pancake through the pool of syrup on her plate.

Her mom shook her head. "Not really," she said. "I lean on them and they take care of me, even when

I don't need it. They were there for us when we did need it, but we're better now. I'm better. And I think it's time for them to have a little peace and quiet."

Josie drew in a sharp breath. "They don't like living with us?"

Her mom reached across the table and patted her hand. "No, sweets, they love having us, don't worry," she said. "It's just, it's time for me to stand on my own two feet, to be independent. And to take care of you."

"And Clementine," Josie added automatically. Her mind was racing as she considered all that this would mean, but she still saw the corners of her mom's mouth turn down the slightest bit at the mention of her dog. "I mean, I'll take care of Clementine," Josie said quickly. Her mom had been clear from day one that if Josie wanted to take in a puppy, then she needed to be responsible for it.

"I know it's a lot to think about," her mom said. "But it's exciting. I've already started looking around with a real estate agent, trying to find a place that's just right for us." Again the corners of her mouth sagged the smallest bit. "It's a little tough to find something in our price range, but I know we will eventually. And you'll have a whole new room to decorate."

Josie liked her own room just fine. And the thought

of moving made her shiver, like a frigid breeze had blown into the diner. But her mom was looking at her hopefully, so Josie did what she could to smile. "It'll be great," she said.

She just hoped it would be true.

• • • ⋈ • • •

Monday, December 12

THE NEXT AFTERNOON, Josie heard the clicking of Ms. D'Amato's high heels coming down the hall a moment before the volunteer coordinator walked into the lounge. "Hi, guys," she said to Josie and Oscar, and, of course, Clementine, who bounded over to greet her. "How's it going?" She was looking at Oscar in particular as she patted Clementine.

Oscar shrugged. "Okay," he said. He was already dressed in his costume, though today he was wearing a black wool hat instead of a baseball cap.

"Well, I hear good things about Santa's Secret Agent," Ms. D'Amato said with a wink.

Oscar couldn't help grinning at that.

"Josie, did you get that list of past Festival performers I sent you?" Ms. D'Amato asked.

"Yes, thanks," Josie said. The list only had two

peds performers Josie hadn't yet asked. One had left the hospital. The other was Dr. Scott, who Josie had asked on her way in. Dr. Scott was happy to help, which was great. But that still left seven acts to find and barely any time to find them—and that was if Josie could even get herself to start approaching non–peds staff without having a complete heart attack.

"I hope you don't mind, but I sent out an email asking for volunteers," Ms. D'Amato said. "I'm not supposed to send mass messages, but I figured this was a special circumstance." She smiled and Josie grinned back.

"Thanks," Josie said. Maybe the email would get more people.

"Though to be honest, people here don't check their work email that much," Ms. D'Amato said, deflating the little hope Josie had built up. "Still, it seemed worth a try."

"I appreciate it," Josie said.

She suspected the email would be like the sign she'd posted—people wouldn't pay any attention. If she wanted the Festival to happen, she'd have to ask everyone on those lists to perform herself. The problem was, she wasn't sure she could do it. And what would happen then? The answer to that made Josie's insides feel like soggy clumps of newspaper.

"I'll let you know if I get any bites," Ms. D'Amato said. She gave Clementine one last pat before walking out.

"I guess we should go sing for the kids," Josie said. She was wearing her favorite elf costume, the green one with tinsel woven in, making the whole thing glitter, and she'd added a jaunty striped hat. But the thought of no Festival had sucked all the enthusiasm out of her.

"Why do you care about this show so much?" Oscar asked, perching on the arm of the sofa, his long legs sticking out. "The kids get to see singing all the time here, anyway."

"The Festival is different," Josie said immediately.

"How?" Oscar asked. He seemed genuinely curious.

"It's in the auditorium," Josie said. "It's fancy—it's like the kids are going to a famous theater in New York City. The acts are always really good, and the last one is this big carol sing-along where a bunch of kids get to go onstage—it's magical really." Josie remembered past Festivals, one in particular, with feathery snowflakes falling on the stage as children came up to sing under the bright lights in front of everyone. Josie was once one of those kids, her heart full as she sang, forgetting, for a short time, why she was in the hospital at all.

"I still don't get why it matters so much to you," Oscar said, reaching down to scratch Clementine behind her ears. "I mean, I know that it's fun, but is it worth all this hassle?"

Josie pulled at a piece of tinsel on the skirt of her costume, debating whether to tell him. It wasn't something she liked talking about, but then again, if she told him, maybe he'd help despite his feelings about Christmas. So she took a deep breath. "It's kind of what I said to Henry," she said. "When my dad was sick and everything was awful, the volunteers here really cheered me up."

Oscar nodded, and Josie could tell he got it, at least this part. "Everyone kept talking about the Festival and how great it was and I was worried my dad would be too sick to go." It still made Josie's chest ache like a punched bruise when she thought about those last weeks of her dad's life, his face pale against the hospital sheets, his voice no more than a hoarse whisper. "And he really loved Christmas. I knew it meant a lot to him."

Oscar nodded again.

"Anyway, the day came and he'd had a bad night, so the nurses weren't sure he should go," Josie said, remembering. "But he said he wanted to, for me, because he wanted to see me sing up on that stage." Now her throat was tight. "So they figured out a way to take him on a stretcher. I stayed with him the whole time and he loved it. His eyes were shining like they hadn't in weeks, and his face looked like him, the real him, not the sick him."

She glanced at Oscar. He'd taken off the sunglasses and was listening closely, so she continued.

"When I climbed on the stage to join in the sing-along I knew how happy he was," Josie said. "How proud. And I was, too." She paused for a moment, sniffling a bit, and Clementine came over and rubbed her head against Josie's leg. Josie bent down to wrap her arms around her dog. "So now when the Festival happens, it makes me feel like he's here, that he's still with me even if he's gone," she went on. "Which probably sounds stupid but—"

"It doesn't sound stupid," Oscar said. He cleared his throat and seemed focused on a spot over Josie's left shoulder. "And I get why you want the Festival to happen."

"Does that mean that maybe you'll help me?" Josie asked.

"I'll help," someone said.

Josie nearly jumped out of her elf boots; she hadn't realized anyone was listening. But sure enough, Gabby was walking into the volunteer room, looking beautiful as always, even though she was still wearing her hospital gown.

"I'm really good at stuff like this," Gabby went on, smiling at Josie in a way that made her feel like the center of everything.

"Um, okay," Josie mumbled, feeling almost blinded, like she was looking into the sun.

"Great!" Gabby said as though it was Josie doing the favor. "So tell me everything I need to know."

As Josie rattled off the details of the Festival, she couldn't help wondering how much Gabby had heard. The stuff about Josie's dad was private, and she didn't like the idea of someone she barely knew hearing about it. And what had Gabby been doing just hanging out right at the door of the lounge, anyway?

"All right, so we need seven more acts," Gabby said, now all business. "Did you ask everyone on those lists?"

"Um, just the people from the peds ward," Josie said.

"That's it?" Gabby asked, her brows pulling together. "Why not anyone else?"

Josie glanced at Oscar, and she could tell they were thinking the same thing: Gabby was pushy. But maybe pushy was what they needed to make the Festival happen.

"I get kind of shy talking to people I don't know," Josie admitted. She could feel herself blushing, as if to prove the point.

Gabby nodded slowly, and Josie wondered if she was thinking about Josie at school, how meek Josie was and how she tripped over her words when a teacher asked her a question. Josie was embarrassed, but Gabby didn't ask any more about it.

"So that's where we start," Gabby said, tucking a silky curl behind one ear. "With the people on the list. But we don't stop there. We should come up with our own ideas for acts, things we think would be awesome. Then we ask people to help out. It's much harder for people to say no when you present them with a whole idea. And we don't just want a repeat of past Festivals—we want this one to be the best ever."

Gabby was more than pushy—she was a force of nature. But Josie had to admit she liked the idea of putting on the best Festival ever. In fact, she loved it.

"What do you say?" Gabby asked.

Oscar was scowling. Josie did think the whole thing was kind of weird. She didn't get why Gabby cared so much when she'd only been in the hospital a few days and probably had a million better things to do. Why would someone with as many friends as Gabby want to spend time with Josie and Oscar? Plus, Josie couldn't help worrying about how much of her story Gabby had overheard. But none of that mattered as much as the Festival, so she nodded.

"Let's do it," she said.

Chapter 13

Monday, December 12

Gabby made her way over to the sofa in the small hospital volunteer room. She was eager to sit down after standing in the hall for so long, listening in on Josie and Oscar. It had been pure luck that she'd walked by just in time to hear Josie's story about the Festival. Well, pure luck and the fact that Gabby had been stalking them a bit. With everything she'd worked for at risk, it was time for something more powerful than her usual charm: She had to find some way to get Josie and Oscar to need her, and need her fast. And since she was going back to school tomorrow, that meant this afternoon was her one shot. The only way to figure out how to become indispensable was to listen in on them, and it had worked—she'd uncovered the necessary information. Now she just had to make sure to use it to her advantage.

"Let's start making a list," Gabby said. "We should put down the acts we have and then start thinking about who to ask next."

"Sounds good," Josie said, her voice so quiet Gabby could barely hear.

"I don't have my cell phone, so can you write it down?" Gabby asked. "Start with who we have so far."

"Some of the high school volunteers are going to do a skit," Josie said, the bells on her shoes jangling as she came to sit down next to Gabby. At school, Josie was a timid mouse, so seeing her all decked out was a bit of a shock. "Nurse Joe is doing a skit, too, with some other nurses from the ward. And I just got Dr. Scott to sign up. She and her husband will dress up as reindeer and sing 'Rudolph.'"

Apparently Josie wasn't the only one going overboard with the Christmas thing here at the hospital.

"That sounds, ah, festive," Gabby said. "Let's write it all down."

Josie pulled out her phone and began typing into it. "Okay, I have our list so far," she said after a moment. "What's next?"

"I have an idea," Oscar said. The way the sides of his mouth pinched together told Gabby he did not care for how she was taking over.

"Sure, what is it?" Gabby asked, smiling warmly. She didn't want Oscar to feel like his toes were getting stepped on, though it didn't seem like he'd done much to help Josie. Not that she was going to point that out.

"I was thinking we should organize a sibling act," he said. "Kids like Henry, who are here a lot and know everyone."

"I love that idea!" Josie exclaimed. "And so will Henry. We can ask Freddy's older brother, too."

"And there must be others," Gabby said. "I bet my brothers would join in."

"They're really cute," Josie said. She grinned. "And high energy."

Gabby couldn't help grinning back. "Yeah," she said. "I can work on that act." Gabby wasn't interested in actually performing, but organizing the kids to do something boisterous and fun would be a blast.

"I'm doing it," Oscar announced. "It was my idea." He looked at Gabby with a raised eyebrow, as if daring her to disagree.

Which figured. Gabby remembered the way he'd hogged the ball in basketball games last year, never letting anyone else shoot so that he'd have the best record at the end of the season. That was probably why he wasn't on the team now—no one wanted to play with someone so selfish. He was also the guy who never helped out with group projects and the lab partner who dumped all the work on the other person. Obviously, he wasn't going to do much to help with the Festival, unless he got into a power struggle with her and had to prove he was right. So she nodded enthusiastically.

"That would be awesome," she said, mentally planning to figure out the skit herself when he dropped out because it was too much work. "So that's set. Who should we ask from the list?"

"Definitely Dr. Wu from OB-GYN," Josie said, typing the name into her phone. "Two years ago he did a juggling act with plastic candy canes while he sang 'Grandma Got Run Over by a Reindeer.'"

"Sounds like a winner," Oscar muttered, and Gabby bit back a grin. Clearly Oscar was not into going overboard about the holidays.

Josie took a moment to glare at him, then continued. "Also, the last act is always a big Christmas carol sing-along, so we just need to find someone to lead that. Last year Dr. Erlan did it, but he got a job in Hawaii or somewhere, so we need to find someone else. And we need to ask the cafeteria workers to perform. They do a big band thing with a brass section and a mini drum line."

"That actually sounds pretty good," Oscar said.

"Yeah," Gabby said. It certainly sounded a lot better than the candy cane juggler. She shifted slightly on the sofa. Her meds seemed stable, but she was still tired from the days in the hospital bed. "Let's start by working on these four acts. After we have them all set up, we can figure out who else to ask."

"It's a plan," Josie agreed happily.

Gabby stood up. "Let's go."

"Wait, right now?" Josie asked. Her cheeks looked pale, like Gabby had suggested facing down a pack of zombies. "I'm not sure I'm ready."

Gabby wasn't sure if Josie would ever be ready, given how anxious she looked.

"Don't worry, I've got it," she said warmly, covering up her impatience flawlessly. She led the way out of the lounge and nearly walked into a stretcher being pushed down the hall with a little girl lying on top.

"Josie! Santa's Secret Agent!" the girl cried out happily. "I'm going home in the morning, so you have to come see me now."

"We'll be there soon, Rosie," Josie said, sounding like a totally different person than the hesitant girl in the volunteer room. "And we're so glad you're well enough to go home." She kicked up her feet, making her shoes jingle merrily.

Rosie waved as the nurse pushed her down the hall with its cheery colored lights blinking. And coming the other way was someone pushing a cart filled with meal trays that were clearly going back to the cafeteria.

"That guy must work in the cafeteria," Gabby said. "Let's go ask him." She headed down the hall without waiting for a response, and Josie and Oscar trailed after her. The worker had stopped at the nurse's station to chat and Gabby marched up to him. The nurse's station had Christmas figures on the counter and a cheerfully decorated tree. Gabby had to admit that the staff did a great job making the hospital look more like a cozy café than a place for sick people. It even smelled like pine and cinnamon. Still, she couldn't wait to get out of there and back to her regular life. But first things first.

"Hi, I'm Gabby," she said, giving the worker her dazzling smile. "This is Oscar and Josie," she paused, noticing that Josie was hiding behind Oscar. "And we have something to ask you."

"Fire away," the worker said. He was short, with gray hair and a bit of a potbelly. Not how Gabby imagined a musician looked. She hoped he was the right person to ask.

"Last year a group of workers from the cafeteria brought down the house with a big band number at the Christmas Festival," Gabby said. "Were you involved? We were hoping you guys could do it again this year."

"Sure," the guy said. "I lead the drum line, and I know everyone would be up for it. I'm Orson Matthews, by the way."

"Excellent," Gabby said, shaking his hand. "I'm Gabby Chavez. Nice to meet you." She was slightly surprised someone so old could lead something as hip as a drum line, but what mattered was that they had another act, and a good one at that.

"Wow, that was fantastic," Josie said as the three of them walked down the hall. Her cheeks were pink again. "Thank you so much."

Even Oscar looked appreciative of Gabby's handiwork. Or at least not as sullen as he'd looked before. Which meant that now was the time.

Gabby took a deep breath, her palms prickling with sweat and her heart beating just a little faster. "You're welcome," she said. "And actually, I have a small favor I want to ask you guys."

Josie nodded, though her brows crinkled a bit. Oscar's lips pursed like he'd sipped a glass of lemonade that was missing the sugar.

But Gabby forged on. "It's just, my sickness," she said, then forced herself to say the word. "My *epilepsy*, is private. So I was hoping you guys wouldn't mind keeping it to yourselves and, you know, not telling anyone at school." She held her breath as she waited for them to answer because this was it, this was her big plan to keep her secret safe: help Josie and Oscar so much that they'd want to help her right back.

Oscar shrugged. "Sure," he said, sounding bored.

"Yeah, no problem," Josie said. There was a slight wrinkle on her forehead, as if she was wondering about Gabby's request, but she had said yes and that was what mattered.

Gabby let out the breath. "Thanks," she said, already planning out her next move. Because it was great that they'd agreed, but the work had just started. Gabby needed to make this Festival the merriest Christmas event of the decade. That way Josie and Oscar would be so impressed, so grateful, that they wouldn't even think to tell people that they'd seen Gabby collapsed on the floor.

They'd happily keep her secret forever.

And Gabby would do everything and anything to make that happen.

Chapter 14

Tuesday, December 13

The halls of Frost Ridge Middle School were packed with kids yelling, laughing, and pushing their way toward the big metal doors and the freedom beyond. It had begun to snow during fifth period, so people were especially eager to get to Sutter Hill for sledding and snowball fights. Normally, Josie hung back after the final bell, waiting for the crowd to thin out before attempting to leave. But today she pushed her way forward.

She was hoping to find Oscar and Gabby so they could start figuring out their plan of attack for the afternoon. She'd almost considered trying to talk to them at lunch but chickened out at the last minute. What if they ignored her? That's what everyone else did—which was why Josie always ate in the library, sneaking in a sandwich that Ms. Murphy, the understanding librarian, pretended not to notice. It would have been awful to approach Oscar or Gabby and have them brush her off, so Josie had stuck to her usual routine. But now, since they were all heading to the same place, it made sense to go together. Didn't it? For a moment Josie wavered and stepped back. Something mushed under her foot.

"Hey, watch it," Aisha said sharply.

Josie looked down—she'd stepped on Aisha's silky black scarf and pulled it onto the floor. "I'm so sorry," Josie said, the words a feeble whimper in her ears. If only she could wear her elf costume or be Mrs. Claus with the shiny black boots at school. Then she would speak up. But obviously only a complete freak would do that, and Josie was close enough to freak status as it was.

"Just be more careful," Aisha said, her voice chilly. She didn't even bother looking at Josie. She just grabbed her scarf and walked away with her group of friends. Luckily, Gabby wasn't among them. If Gabby had seen that, she'd probably have second thoughts about helping with the Festival, and Josie couldn't let that happen. She needed Gabby to pull it off.

A group of boys talking loudly about the basketball game over the weekend passed by. Oscar was at the edge of the group, his black hair flying all over the place. He glanced over and saw Josie standing there.

Feeling silly, Josie raised her hand and waved. Oscar nodded, the way he did when they passed at school, then continued on with his friends.

"Hey, Oscar, wait," Josie said.

But her whispery voice didn't carry across the loud conversations around them, and Oscar headed for the exit without her.

Josie bit her lip, telling herself that he just hadn't heard and that he wanted some time with his friends. But even so, the brush-off stung.

"Hey, Josie," Gabby said, coming up behind her. Gabby was alone, which was weird. She was never alone.

"Why aren't you with your friends?" Josie blurted out. Ugh, it was good that people ignored her at school—whenever she opened her mouth, something stupid came out.

"I told them I had stuff to do after school," Gabby said, giving Josie her luminous smile.

Josie wondered if Gabby'd told her friends that the stuff involved Josie, but then she pushed the thought aside. It didn't matter—what mattered was the Festival.

"So I'm thinking we go straight to Dr. Wu and try to sign him up," Gabby said, leading the way through the doors. Josie fell into step next to her, nodding as

Gabby mapped out the plan. There was an arctic wind whipping the falling snow, the flakes crusty with ice as they hit Josie's cheeks. After the steamy warmth of the hall, the cold was revitalizing, but by the time they'd reached the path, Josie was fumbling in her pockets for her mittens and hat.

"Oh, and this time you can't hide when I ask," Gabby said.

"You saw that?" Josie asked sheepishly.

Gabby laughed. "It was pretty hard to miss." She straightened her maroon scarf that matched her maroon cloche hat and went perfectly with her navy peacoat. Josie felt like a butterball next to her in her huge down jacket.

"Talking to people I don't know isn't really my strong suit," Josie said. "I appreciate you helping us out with it. The Festival means a lot to me—and to all the kids stuck in the hospital for the holidays." She pressed her mouth into a line so she wouldn't babble on. Gabby, with her shiny hair, fabulous outfits, and confident charm, made her nervous.

Gabby bit her lip for a moment but then smiled her dazzling smile. "I'm happy to do it," she said. "And I'm sure we'll find our ten acts."

"I really hope so," Josie said. "A lot of people are away, though, or have plans already. And then there are people like me who want to help but aren't performers." Then the obvious occurred to her: Gabby was comfortable anywhere and would probably be great up on the stage. "Maybe *you* could do something," she said as they stopped on the corner. A snowplow was driving by, and they stepped back to avoid being hit by the spray of snow flying up beside it. "Do you sing or act or anything?"

Gabby shook her head. "That's not really my thing," she said. "I don't have talent like that. But I'll help organize and maybe I could go with you to visit the kids in their rooms sometime. I like playing silly games with my brothers, and it seems like that's kind of what you guys do."

"Sure, anytime," Josie said, though it was pretty impossible to imagine sleek, poised Gabby singing goofy songs. She'd probably offered just to be nice. Though why she was being so nice still puzzled Josie.

They'd reached Dandelion Drive. "I need to run and get my dog," Josie said. She wasn't sure if she should invite Gabby to her house—it wasn't like they were friends exactly. And thinking about showing someone her house reminded Josie that it might not be home for much longer—that she and her mom might be finding a new place to live. That was something she didn't like thinking about at all. So it was better if she could just dash in quickly for Clementine and then head to the hospital.

"Okay, I'll see you in the volunteer room," Gabby said easily. "And we can go find Dr. Wu then. Maybe a couple of other people, too. We don't have much time to find four more acts."

"Sounds good," Josie said. In fact, it sounded great as long as Gabby was doing the asking. "We'll get Oscar and then go to OB-GYN."

"Right," Gabby said.

Josie thought she saw Gabby roll her eyes, but she wasn't sure. So she took off for her house, eager to get to the hospital and get the remaining acts they needed to make the Festival happen.

BOTH GABBY AND Oscar were in the volunteer lounge when Josie arrived. Josie quickly shed her outside layers and settled Clementine on the sofa to wait until they were back. Then the three of them headed to the OB-GYN ward.

"Hi, we're here to see Dr. Wu," Gabby told the woman at the nurse's station.

Oscar was fiddling with a bowl of peppermints on the counter, and Josie made a concentrated effort not to inch behind him.

"I'm sorry, kids. Dr. Wu is in Sierra Leone with Doctors Without Borders until March," the nurse at the station said. "Can I get another doctor for you?"

Josie sagged against the counter in defeat, but Gabby flashed the nurse her famous smile. "Actually, maybe you can help us," she said, her voice sweet and peppy. "We're signing up volunteers for the Christmas Festival, and we need awesome people like you to perform."

The nurse smiled. "I'm already part of the show!" she said. "A couple of us from OB-GYN are doing the 'Night Before Christmas' skit with Nurse Joe. He's got a whole group participating."

Josie's heart sank. Right then, Oscar somehow managed to spill the mints all over the counter and hastily began scooping them back into the bowl. Josie leaned over to help, glad for a distraction. Luckily, they were individually wrapped.

"Oh, that's great," Gabby said, shooting Oscar an evil glare that the nurse couldn't see. "Do you think any of the doctors might want to sign up, too?"

"I can ask," the nurse said. "But honestly we're pretty short-staffed around the holidays, and you never know when a patient is going to come in to have a baby. The doctors here might not be the best ones to ask because if a baby's coming and there are any problems, it's all hands on deck."

"Well, thanks so much, anyway," Gabby said.

Josie couldn't help admiring how warm Gabby was, even though they'd gotten bad news. Gabby really was a pro at this life skill. And every other one, too, it seemed.

"Okay, that was disappointing, but we'll find a replacement," Gabby said as they walked down the hall. "And next time keep your hands off the mints," she told Oscar.

"It wasn't my fault," Oscar said. "I think there was something wrong with the bowl."

"You sound just like my little brothers," Gabby huffed.

Josie wanted to talk about their new game plan: She had really been counting on Dr. Wu and wasn't sure who was going to take his place. But Gabby was charging ahead, annoyed at Oscar, and Oscar was sulking about the mints, so Josie followed along silently. They could figure it out upstairs.

The OB-GYN unit was painted a cheery yellow and had murals of storks and chubby-cheeked babies.

But as soon as they left that wing and were back on the main hall, it was beige walls and tasteful land-scapes. Josie liked the murals better and was glad when they turned onto the peds ward, with its col-ored lights and big tree.

"It's Reindeer Day," Nurse Joe announced when he saw them, pointing to the antlers on his head. "Grab a pair." He gestured to a cardboard box at the nurse's station that was half-filled with plush antler headbands strung with bells.

Josie picked one up and slid it on. She assumed Gabby would pass—the headband would probably mess up her hair—but Gabby surprised her by imme-diately grabbing a pair and perching them on her head.

"What about yours?" Gabby asked Oscar.

Oscar shook his head. "I don't do Christmas cos-tumes," he said.

Josie thought she heard Gabby mutter, "it figures," but when she looked at Gabby, she was just nodding politely.

"Josie, Oscar, come sing for us," Henry called, poking his head out of Melanie's room.

"Sure," Josie said. The Festival would have to wait. They needed to see the kids first. "Just let me get Clementine." She hurried back to the volunteer room.

Clementine was curled up on the sofa, but she gave a happy bark when Josie walked in and bounded over on her fat fuzzy paws.

"I missed you, too," Josie told her dog. She knelt down to scratch Clementine's ears and then pressed her face against the dog's soft fur. There was really nothing better than her wriggly, downy Clementine.

But Henry and Melanie were waiting, so Josie made a quick dash into the costume closet for a reindeer costume to go with her antlers, zipped herself into it, and walked back to the others with Clementine.

"I brought your costume," she said to Oscar, handing him his cap and sunglasses, which he slipped on.

"Hey, guys," Jade said as she and Ed walked past. They were dressed as elves but of course had their reindeer headbands on, too.

"Should I come in with you guys?" Gabby asked, tugging on a curl.

"Definitely," Josie said, sounding much more confident than she felt. She really didn't see Gabby fitting in with what they did. And Josie didn't want to feel self-conscious with the kids the way she had back when Oscar was "observing." But she couldn't say no, so the three of them walked in.

Melanie lay on the bed attached to tubes and wires that connected to beeping machines. Her skin was waxy and had a grayish tinge, but her brown eyes lit up when she saw them. Clementine walked over, her tail wagging, and put her paws up on the bed so she could lick Melanie's hand. Melanie petted Clementine for a moment, then let her hand rest on the dog's head. Clementine seemed to know that Melanie did not have the energy for a vigorous ear rub—she simply held still, allowing Melanie's hand to stay in place.

"This is Gabby," Josie said, first to Melanie and then to Henry and their mom. She sat by the bed while Henry bounced around the room like a windup toy that couldn't stop.

"Sing 'Rudolph' because you're reindeer!" he shouted.

"You've got it," Josie said, and launched into a rousing rendition of the song. Oscar sang along a little hesitantly, and after a moment Gabby joined in, too. At first she was quiet. But to Josie's surprise, her voice got louder as the song went on. When Henry began dancing around, Gabby joined him. Josie would have imagined Gabby's dancing to be graceful and smooth like everything else she did, but she couldn't have been more wrong. Gabby was giggling wildly, waving her arms about and stomping her feet. She looked like a cross between a monkey and a dinosaur. Josie blinked a few times, almost messing up the song, but it really was Gabby Chavez acting like a complete goof.

"More!" Henry shouted when the song and dance had ended. His cheeks were flushed, and he looked nothing like the sad boy from a few weeks before.

"Remember to ask nicely," Henry's mom said. But she was smiling, too.

"Can you please sing about Harold's angels?" Henry asked. "That's Melanie's favorite."

Melanie grinned at her brother. "It is," she told them.

"I don't really know the words to that one," Gabby said. "Just the chorus."

She was breathing hard from the dance and looked ready for a rest. Josie remembered she had been in the hospital not so long ago and probably still needed to take it easy.

"Me neither," Oscar said. He was fiddling with his cap.

"No problem," Josie said. The song was one of her favorites, too, and now that Gabby had revealed her true silly nature, Josie was fine singing alone. She began, letting her voice soar on the high notes, trilling where it felt right.

When she was done, everyone burst into applause.

Josie ducked her head, feeling thankful for the costume. "Okay, we'll let you get some rest," she said, and led the way out of Melanie's room.

"Why aren't you singing in the Festival?" Gabby demanded the second they were out in the hall.

Josie's chest tightened—she did not want to have this conversation. "I don't like singing in front of groups," she said.

"Well, you're going to have to get over it," Gabby said, as if Josie's fear was like a flat tire that could be fixed right up. "You are an incredible singer and owe it to everyone here to share that. Plus, then we'll only need three more acts."

Nothing was going to get Josie to agree to sing, not even Gabby Chavez. It wasn't worth wasting time on when she had other matters to discuss. "You should be the one to perform," she said. "You made Henry's day with your dancing."

Gabby's cheeks began turning pink. "Yeah, I can get kind of carried away with stuff like that," she said. "But me dancing around like a crazy girl onstage isn't exactly an act."

Even Oscar had to laugh at that.

"You could do a fun skit, like 'The Grinch,'" Josie said, waving to Nurse Joe as he walked by. "That's my favorite Christmas story and you'd be a great Grinch."

"Actually, that seems more like Oscar's skill set," Gabby said, then bit her lip like she hadn't meant to say something so sharp.

Oscar's eyes narrowed.

"Either of you guys would be fabulous in it," Josie said quickly, not wanting a fight.

But both of them were shaking their heads.

"I'm doing the sibling act," Oscar reminded them sullenly.

"Have you started organizing it?" Gabby asked.

Oscar spun to face her. "I'm working on it," he said shortly. "But I think Josie's right—you'd be a perfect Grinch."

"You guys, the Grinch is the best," Josie said, upset they were bickering and annoyed neither of them saw the awesomeness of the Grinch. "His heart grows in the end and he saves Christmas—there's nothing better than that."

"I like the Grinch," Gabby said with a smile that was tight along the edges. "But I'm not a stage per-former. I'm more of a small group entertainer. Not like you with that incredible voice."

And now they were back to that, but Josie had an idea on how to get out of it. She took out her phone and pulled up her list. "We've asked everyone we thought of so far," she said. "We need some new people to ask."

Gabby was nodding, but she was looking up at the clock over the nurse's station. "Sorry, I need to get going. Let's all think about it tonight. We need three more acts plus someone to lead the carol sing-along, and we have to get you to sign up, Josie. So that's the agenda for tomorrow."

Josie didn't care for the last item, and she was also worried they were still so many acts short. There were only seven days left until their deadline. What if they couldn't find the acts plus a sing-along leader in time? But she couldn't pressure Gabby to stay, not when she probably had things to do at home or was feeling tired after her stay in the hospital. So she waved good-bye, and she and Oscar continued along the peds ward, visiting each kid there.

"HOW ARE THINGS at home?" Josie asked an hour later. She, Oscar, and Clementine were on the sofa in the volunteer room. Clementine had stretched out so that her head was on Oscar's knee but most of her furry body rested against Josie. Oscar scratched behind her ears while Josie rubbed her back, and the dog closed her eyes with a squeak of contentment.

Oscar shrugged. "Not great," he said. "I'll be glad when Christmas is over." His voice was heavy, and when she heard it, Clementine snuggled in closer to him.

"That's rough," Josie said, her heart aching for Oscar. She hated to think of Oscar not having any Christmas fun when everything about the holiday made her so happy. Maybe the Festival would help. As long as they managed to make it happen. She was about to ask what his ideas were for the sibling act and who else they might ask, when Clementine sat up straight. She sniffed, then padded over to the door just as it opened.

"Mom," Josie exclaimed, surprised to see her mom, still in work clothes, walk in.

"Hey, sweetie," her mom said, bending down to scratch Clementine's ears. "I got off a little early and thought I'd swing by so we could walk home together."

"That's nice," Josie said, standing up. It was more than nice; it was strange. Josie couldn't remember her mom ever just "swinging by" before. But she wasn't going to ask about it now, not with Oscar right there. So she gathered her manners and gestured toward her new friend. "Mom, this is Oscar."

Josie's mom stuck out her hand, which Oscar awkwardly accepted. "Nice to meet you," he mumbled. He looked slightly panicked when Josie headed to the costume closet to change back into her clothes. Clearly talking to grown-ups wasn't his thing. But her mom began asking about the patients they'd seen that day, and pretty soon Oscar sounded normal again. And when Josie came out of the closet she saw why: He was sitting on the sofa with Clementine settled on his lap. Even more proof that her dog was amazing.

A few minutes later, Josie headed out into the snowy afternoon with her mom and Clementine. The sidewalk was covered with fresh drifts and walking was a bit tricky, though Josie loved the squelching feeling of stepping down on piles of fresh snow.

"I have some good news," her mom said in a voice that sounded oddly flat and not good-newsy at all.

"Okay," Josie said uncertainly.

"I found an apartment," her mom went on as they stopped at the corner and waited for a car to pass. "Given our budget restrictions and how tight the real estate market is, we're lucky to have come across it. It's big and bright, not too far from Grandma and Grandpa's, and right down the street from the park."

So that was why her mom sounded so hesitant: They were going to have to move.

"It sounds good," Josie said. Her feet were heavy in her big boots, and the wind was making her eyes water. Josie knew she had to be a good sport for her mom's sake—this meant so much to her—but Josie *really* didn't want to move.

"There's just one thing," Josie's mom said, and now her voice was downright foreboding. "This building doesn't accept pets."

Everything in Josie froze colder than the mounds of icy snow around them.

"So we have a choice to make," her mother went on. "We can take this apartment and find a new home for Clementine, or we wait to move."

The words sliced into Josie, cutting deep. "So if we take the apartment, we'd have to give up Clementine?" she asked, hoping maybe she'd misunderstood.

"Yes," her mom said, dashing her hopes. "I just haven't seen any other apartments available that are right for us and that I can afford. So if we give up this one, we might have to wait a year or two while I build up some more savings."

"Could Clementine stay with Grandma and Grandpa?" Josie asked in a small voice. She wasn't sure she could bear even that, but her mom shook her head.

"They're just too old to walk a dog regularly," her mom said. "I'm sure we could find someone loving to take Clementine in—she's such a sweetie. But, hon, it's up to you. I can't make you give her up when you've taken such good care of her all these years. So if it's too much, you say the word and we stay." Josie could hear the hope in her mother's voice, how much it meant to her to move. But there at Josie's feet was her dog, her loyal companion and best friend for more than five years.

How could Josie possibly choose between them?

Chapter 15

Tuesday, December 13

"Hi, Oscar," Oscar's mom said, bustling in the front door. "I didn't have time to make dinner, so I got takeout from Danny's. Would you set the table?"

Oscar was in the living room doing homework at the old-fashioned desk that had once belonged to his grandfather. "Sure," he said, closing his math book. The smell of food made him hungry, and he hurried to set out plates, silverware, and glasses for everyone.

He and his mom were unpacking the warm cardboard containers when his dad walked in. "I thought you were cooking tonight," he said.

Oscar's gut began to fill with acid as his mom narrowed her eyes.

"Hello to you, too," she said coldly. "I didn't have time to cook."

"We don't have the money for endless takeout, Marlene," his dad said, loosening his tie.

"I know, but we needed to eat something," his mother said. She slammed a carton on the table, and the top bounced off. Chili oozed over the sides.

"It takes ten minutes to whip up an omelet," his father said, grabbing a napkin to mop up the chili.

"Are you offering to come home and cook one?" his mom seethed. "Because it's actually a little more work than that."

"I can't cook during the week," his father barked. "You know that. It's one of the few things you—"

"Stop," his mother said. Normally, this was the point where she'd be yelling. Instead, her voice was quiet. She sat down and put her head in her hands.

For one horrible moment, Oscar thought she was crying.

But then she looked up, her eyes dark as she gazed at Oscar's dad. "I can't do this," she said.

"Marlene we agreed to wait until—" his dad started, but his mom was shaking her head.

"What's the point?" she asked. "We agreed to wait so that the holidays wouldn't be spoiled for Oscar. But us arguing every second—that's even worse."

Oscar stepped back, instinctively holding up his hands to protect himself from what was coming. But his hands did nothing to stop the pain of his mother's next statement.

"Oscar, your dad and I are separating," she said, the words biting into him with sharp fangs. "He already found an apartment, and he'll be moving out January first."

"Why can't you work it out?" Oscar asked, his voice wobbling dangerously. "You always tell me to work it out when I get into fights."

"Sweetie, we tried," his mom said in a tired voice. "But things between adults get complicated."

There was nothing complicated about the fact that Oscar would be starting the new year with a busted-up family, a thought that made him want to punch something. Only for some reason instead of punching, he was crying. It was stupid and babyish, and yet he couldn't stop.

"Oh, Oscar," his mom said, reaching for him as her voice cracked.

But Oscar wasn't having any of it.

He flew from the room as his parents called after him, up the stairs and into the bathroom, the only place in the house with a lock. Which he locked. And then he turned on the bathwater so his parents, who were already knocking on the door outside, could not hear how this had broken him.

Chapter 16

Wednesday, December 14

Gabby strode into the lounge. "I have good news and bad," she said. "Which do you want first?"

Gabby had gone to ask the last three performers on the list if they'd be willing to sign up for the Festival while Josie, Oscar, and Clementine had visited a new patient.

"The bad news," Josie said. She was a big believer in getting bad things over with. Well, unless the bad thing was a horrible choice between her mom and her dog. That was something she was putting off as long as she could. It helped to have the Festival plans to distract her.

"None of the people on the list can do it," Gabby said. "They're all going away for the holidays."

Josie's shoulders sagged in her plush Mrs. Claus costume. "That's *really* bad news. Is the good news that you signed up three replacements?"

"It's not that good," Gabby said, sitting down on the chair. "But I did get an idea for who to ask next."

Josie looked over at Oscar, who had been quiet since they arrived. Clementine was curled up in his lap, and Oscar was resting his hands on her soft tan fur.

"Okay, what's the idea?" Josie asked.

"When I was walking back, I saw two of the janitors cleaning up a spill in the main hall," Gabby said, pulling out her phone. She'd taken over responsibility for the list. "And I realized we should ask some of them to perform."

"Good thinking," Josie said. She couldn't remember if any of the janitors had been in the Festival before, but they tended to be pretty friendly and seemed like a good department to approach.

"We could ask them to do 'The Gift of the Magi,'" Gabby said. "That's kind of a classic."

"I love that story," Josie agreed. She glanced at Oscar, who smiled weakly. Something was clearly wrong, but it was just as clear that he didn't want to talk about it. "And I had an idea for an act, too."

"Oh, great," Gabby said. "What?"

"I was thinking we could ask some of the X-ray technicians to do a skeleton Christmas skit," Josie said, playing with her fuzzy costume cuff. She kind of missed Clementine cuddling with her, but clearly her dog knew that Oscar was sad and needed some snuggling. "I think a lot of the little kids would love something that was a little scary but also funny like that." She'd come up with the idea when she'd seen Dr. Scott with an envelope of X-rays. She hoped it didn't sound stupid.

"That's fabulous!" Gabby said. "I'm writing it down." She paused two seconds to type into her phone. "Let's go ask them both."

"Um, I was thinking maybe you could ask while we go perform for the kids," Josie said. She didn't want to be too needy since Gabby was already helping so much. But it always went so well when Gabby was the one making the request.

"Don't you think you should try asking?" Gabby asked.

Josie didn't think so at all.

"It could be good practice, talking to a few people you don't know now, then singing at the show later," Gabby said.

Josie didn't understand why Gabby wanted her to perform so much. "It's a pretty big leap to talk to one person and then sing to five hundred of them," she pointed out.

"The first steps are the hardest but the most important," Gabby said. "Just try."

Josie wasn't sure how to get out of it. She shot a pleading glance Oscar's way, but he barely looked up and seemed to miss her distress. "I'll stay here with Clementine," he said.

She was stuck. But at least she was half-hidden in the baggy folds of the velvety Mrs. Claus costume. "Okay," she said, standing up.

Gabby led the way into the hall where the two janitors were done cleaning. One was setting up a caution sign over the wet spot on the floor while the other was wringing out the mop.

Josie's feet slowed as they got close. Gabby poked her in the back and Josie jumped. Gabby had sharp fingers.

"Hi," Josie said as they came up to the workers, the butterflies starting in her chest and making it hard to get enough air. "I'm Josie, and I—"

"Josie's my girl," Nurse Joe called out as he sailed by pushing a smiling Melanie in a wheelchair. "And you too, Gabs."

Josie saw Gabby grin at the nickname but then refocus her attention. Worried she was about to get another poke, Josie continued. "Um, we wondered if you guys might—The Christmas Festival, the one here at the hospital." She faltered.

One guy glanced at the other, and both looked concerned that Josie was ill. Or insane. Or both.

"We need volunteers," Josie practically wheezed. Then she felt a hand on her arm.

"We're signing people up to perform in the Christmas Festival," Gabby said smoothly, putting Josie out of her misery. "And we wondered if a group of you guys might be willing to do a skit of 'The Gift of the Magi.'"

"Sure," the first janitor said, sticking out his hand. "I'm Chris, and this is Zuri. I'm no actor, but this guy takes classes at the college. You do some drama, right?"

"Yeah," Zuri said with an easy smile. "And I'd love to round up some of our crew to help you out."

"Fabulous," Gabby said, beaming at them. She whipped out her phone to add them to the list while the two workers headed off.

"Sorry about that," Josie said weakly. Her face was still on fire from the mortifying incident.

"Yeah, that was kind of a disaster," Gabby said. The words were blunt, but she was looking at Josie sympathetically. "I guess I didn't realize how hard it would be for you."

"So now you'll do the asking?" Josie asked. She

was sure Gabby would say yes now that she'd seen what a failure Josie was.

But Gabby was shaking her head. "The only way to get over a fear like this is to confront it," she said. "You are definitely going to be doing the asking from now on."

"But we won't get any more volunteers," Josie wailed. "I'll scare everyone off."

Gabby laughed. "No, you'll learn how to put together a sentence even when you're nervous. And then you'll thank me for changing your life."

"Josie, Gabby, come sing," Henry called from down the hall.

Josie glanced up at the clock. "Kids are waiting for us," she said. "We should probably go perform."

"Okay, but you're not leaving this hospital until we talk to the X-ray techs," Gabby said.

They headed back to the lounge. Josie assumed they were just going for Clementine and Oscar, but as soon as they got there, Gabby headed for the costume closet. "Help me pick something fun," she said to Josie.

Josie looked at Oscar, sure he'd be as taken aback by this as she was. But he was still slumped on the sofa cuddling Clementine.

"Sure," Josie said. She followed Gabby into the closet, where she figured Gabby would choose one of the more elegant outfits, like the shimmery angel gown. But after going through the rack, Gabby held up a brightly striped candy cane outfit bedecked with bells. "What do you think?" she asked.

"I think I can't believe that Gabby Chavez, queen of the sixth grade, would ever wear something like that," Josie said. As soon as the words were out, Josie pressed her lips together. But of course it was too late.

Gabby was silent for a moment, and Josie could feel herself shrinking down in her costume. She'd probably ruined everything with her thoughtless remark. It was true of course, but that just made it worse.

Finally, Gabby gestured to Josie in the Mrs. Claus outfit. "I guess we all have a secret side," she said. "You with that voice of yours. Oscar being a super spy. And me getting silly with little kids."

Josie still couldn't help feeling that there was more to it, but she was going to keep her mouth shut. All that mattered was that Gabby liked helping. Plus, she had a point about the hospital and secrets.

"And really, Aisha's the queen of the sixth grade,"

Gabby added as she pulled on the candy cane costume, which jingled loudly. "I'm just one of the crowd."

It wasn't true, but Josie didn't care. The kids were waiting, and she was ready to sing.

* * * ≺≻ * * *

AN HOUR LATER, they were back. Gabby flopped down on the sofa, clearly tired from all her dancing. Oscar went over to the window and looked out, Clementine at his heels. The little dog had only left his side to greet patients, and now she pressed against him, her short tail wagging. Oscar knelt down so he could give her ears a good rub.

After a moment, Gabby sat up. "So now we need to go to X-ray," she said. "But first I want to know how it's going with the sibling act."

She and Josie looked at Oscar, who obviously hadn't been listening. "What?" he asked, as though coming back from a very faraway place in his mind. Josie figured he was thinking about his parents, and she wished there was something she could say or do to help.

"The sibling act," Gabby said evenly, though she was tugging rather hard on one of her curls and making the bells on her costume ring. "Have you started asking kids or planning what you want the kids to do?"

"Not yet," Oscar said vaguely.

"But we really need to get going on that," Gabby said. "We have to give the final list to Ms. D'Amato in six days. Josie and I are doing everything we can, and you need to help out, too."

Oscar gave Clementine one last pat and then stood up. "I'll take care of it," he said. "But I need to head home now."

Gabby shot him an irritated look. "You can't just stay for five minutes to plan this?"

"No," Oscar said, slipping on his coat and grabbing his backpack. He pushed the door so hard, it triggered the mechanism that kept it wide open, but he didn't stop to close it. He just headed out, his shoulders hunched and his hat pulled low.

"Whatever," Gabby huffed, standing up. She looked at Josie. "Let's go talk to the X-ray technicians."

"Stay," Josie told Clementine, who sat obediently on the sofa. Josie thought about closing the door but figured it would be nice for Clementine to see people passing by, so she left it as it was.

"He's not going to get it done," Gabby complained as they waited for the elevator.

"I think he will," Josie said. She wasn't sure, but she wanted to give Oscar the benefit of the doubt.

Gabby waved a dismissive hand as the elevator doors opened. "It doesn't matter. I'll take care of it if he doesn't."

"I really do think Oscar will handle it," Josie said. "He's just having a bad day today."

"He seems to have those a lot," Gabby said with a sniff.

Obviously, Josie couldn't tell Gabby what was going on with Oscar, but she wished Gabby would be just a bit more understanding.

As they made their way to the X-ray lab, Josie's chest began to fill with butterflies.

"Breathe," Gabby told her. "And imagine that the people you're talking to are naked."

"Ew!" Josie exclaimed.

Gabby giggled. "I read that's what you're supposed to do if you get nervous speaking to big groups," she said. "That way you aren't intimidated by the people you're talking to."

"No, just totally mortified to be in a room full of naked people," Josie said.

Gabby laughed harder, and Josie couldn't help joining in. Gabby was fun. It was hard to imagine that Josie had ever been intimidated by her.

"Okay, this is it," Gabby said as they got to the lab. "You can do it."

Josie wasn't so sure, but she opened the door and walked in. A woman sat at a desk in front of a closed door, behind which Josie figured the actual X-raying took place. The woman was packing up her briefcase, and she frowned slightly when she saw them.

"Yes?" she asked.

Josie took the big breath Gabby had advised and almost choked on it.

"Are you okay?" the woman asked.

"I'm fine," Josie said, her eyes watering. "I'm Josie, and we're here to ask you about the Christmas Festival."

She'd managed a full sentence! But the woman was looking at her blankly.

"Um, every year the hospital has this kind of Festival," Josie said. "It's on Christmas Eve and it's a, uh, Festival with performances and stuff." It was no longer going as well.

The woman tipped her head to the side as she stared at Josie. "I know about the Festival," she said. "Is there a reason you're telling me about it?"

"Yes," Josie said, taking a second to try and calm the butterflies that were beating furiously in her chest. The way the woman was tapping her fingers on the desk impatiently was not helping at all.

"We're signing up performers," Gabby said, nodding at Josie to go on.

"And we wondered if some people in your department," Josie said. "People like you, I mean, would want to help."

"Help backstage?" the woman asked, her brows drawing together.

"We were thinking you could make up a skit about a skeleton Christmas since you guys do stuff with bones." She wanted to cringe at how dumb that sounded, but then the woman actually smiled for the first time.

"Cute idea," she said.

"So you'll do it?" Gabby asked, pulling out the phone.

But the woman shook her head. "I'm more of a backstage person," she said.

Josie's hopes were instantly squashed.

"But I can ask the others," the woman said. "We have a few drama queens around here. Maybe some of them will want to help out."

"Thanks," Josie said, trying to sound appreciative instead of dismal.

"That wasn't bad," Gabby said once they were back in the hall and heading up to the volunteer room.

"You don't have to be nice," Josie said, her feet dragging in her Mrs. Claus boots. "I know I was awful."

"I mean it," Gabby insisted. "You actually managed to ask her, and that's a big deal."

"Except for the part where she said no," Josie said. They were back on the ward, and she was eager to get to her dog. Clementine always made her feel better.

But Gabby put a hand on her arm. "She didn't say no," she corrected. "She was tired and wanted to go home, but she still liked your idea and said she'd ask around. I wouldn't be surprised if she found some people and we actually get our skeleton Christmas skit."

"You really think so?" Josie asked.

Gabby nodded, her face serious. "I do," she said. "And really, Josie, you did a great job asking."

It turned out Gabby could make people feel better, too. Josie was smiling as they headed into the volunteer lounge. But then she looked around, and the smile evaporated. The sofa was empty.

"Where's Clementine?" Josie asked, her throat tightening, her voice shrill.

"I thought she was here," Gabby said, coming in behind Josie. "Did she just go into the closet?"

But Clementine wasn't there.

"She has to be somewhere," Gabby said, resting a hand on Josie's arm. "I bet she just smelled cookies down the hall or something."

Josie's heart was skittering wildly in her chest and it was getting hard to breathe. Clementine always stayed when Josie told her to stay. Always. There was no way she'd just wander off.

"Josie," Gabby said, her voice calm as she looked right into Josie's eyes. "We're going to look for her and we're going to find her."

The soothing way she spoke allowed Josie to take a shaky breath. "Okay," she said.

Gabby headed straight for the nurse's station. "Clementine is missing," she announced to Nurse Joe.

His eyes widened. He turned to the other nurses. "We need to find Clementine ASAP." Then he looked back at Josie and Gabby. "When did you realize she was gone?"

Josie wasn't sure she could talk with her throat squeezed so tight, but it turned out she didn't need to.

"We went down to the X-ray department about twenty minutes ago," Gabby said. "Clementine was on the couch in the volunteer room when we left, but she wasn't there when we got back."

"Could she have somehow opened the door?" Nurse Joe asked.

"The door was wedged open," Gabby said.

There was a tray of gingerbread cookies on the desk next to them, and the smell made Josie's stomach churn. Why hadn't she closed the door when she left Clementine in the lounge? How could she have made such a terrible mistake?

"Okay, so she probably just wandered off," said Nurse Joe. He gave Josie a steady look. "And we're going to search every inch of this place until we track her down."

"We'll help," Jade said, coming up with Ed and leaning over to squeeze Josie's arm. They were dressed in their regular clothes, ready to go home, and Josie was dimly aware that she felt grateful they were staying to search for her dog.

"We're going to find her," Ed said firmly.

Josie nodded, even though she thought she might throw up. Or faint. Or both. But Gabby and Nurse Joe took charge. Calls were placed, and soon every nook and cranny of the hospital had someone assigned to search it for Clementine.

"We're in charge of the peds ward," Gabby announced when everywhere else had been assigned. So she and Josie went into each room, asking all the kids and their parents. But not a single person had seen Clementine.

"I'm sure someone else found her," Gabby said as they went back to the nurse's station thirty long, terrible minutes later. But Josie could hear the waver of doubt in her voice.

The bright colors of the ward had dimmed for Josie, as though she were walking through a gray fog that had seeped into her skin and filled up her chest, making her clammy and cold, inside and out.

"I bet someone found her snacking on treats in the cafeteria, and they're bringing her up right now," Gabby said. But she was pulling on a curl as she spoke, her eyes darting around, looking to see if someone, anyone, was bringing back Clementine.

They stood at the nurse's station, Josie leaning against the desk because it was too much to stand, Gabby with a warm hand resting on her back.

The elevator doors opened, and Nurse Joe stepped out.

Josie drew in a breath, ready to ask, but then she saw his face and that told her everything.

"I'm so sorry, Josie, but Clementine just isn't anywhere in the hospital," he said.

"Then where could she be?" Gabby asked, wrapping an arm around Josie.

"She's gone," Josie said, her voice breaking. "Someone stole Clementine."

And then she burst into tears.

Chapter 17

Thursday, December 15

"Gabby, what do you think?" Jasmine asked.

Gabby and her friends were at their usual prime table in the cafeteria surrounded by loud conversation, laughter from the tables around them, and the overpowering smell of sloppy joes, today's lunch special. Gabby had opted for grilled cheese, but the bread had been over-toasted and was now more like a brick than a sandwich. Gabby wanted to go get something else to eat, but instead she dutifully checked out the sweater Jasmine had picked up at Mulligans and decorated with sequins.

"It looks great," Gabby said, and the others now nodded in agreement. "I love that shade of green."

"I wonder if it would look good on me," Becky mused.

"I don't think so," Aisha said. "Your skin is too washed out."

Becky's face, which had never seemed particularly washed out to Gabby, turned red. Aisha didn't notice but Gabby did and she felt a flash of sympathy for Becky. Aisha was tart—everyone knew that. It was part of what made her fun. But Becky, who was pulling her napkin apart, did not seem to be enjoying herself much right now.

"I really have to get to Mulligans," Isabelle announced. "Let's go tomorrow after school," she said, looking at Gabby. "My mom can drive us."

"Great idea," Aisha said. "Count me in."

Tomorrow Gabby would be at the hospital finding the final acts for the Festival. But of course she couldn't say that. "I have family stuff," she said, adding a note of regret to her voice. "We do a lot around Christmas."

"Maybe we could go sometime over winter break," Isabelle said.

"If you aren't stuck babysitting again," Aisha added, twirling her spoon around in her yogurt.

Yogurt looked good to Gabby, or maybe she just needed a little break from the conversation. She stood up. "I'm going to get more food," she said. "Anyone need anything?"

She hadn't realized how abrupt she'd been until she saw her friends' faces.

"Sorry, I'm just hungry and that sandwich is totally gross," she said, putting on her dazzling smile.

Her friends smiled and all was well. She had taken

care of things. But as she wove through the packed tables, passing a group of girls sneakily looking at a phone and a table of guys building a truly disgusting food sculpture, she couldn't help thinking how tiring it was to be so careful all the time. For a moment she remembered being at the hospital the day before, visiting Melanie and Henry, who had clapped along while Josie and Gabby made up silly verses to "Deck the Halls." That was way more fun than talking about sweaters and watching every word that came out of her mouth.

She paused as she realized that she wasn't being completely open and honest at the hospital, either. Josie and Oscar still didn't know the real reason she had first volunteered to help with the Festival.

There were only a few other students in the buffet area, so Gabby was able to grab a blueberry yogurt and pay pretty fast. As she stepped back into the large sitting area with its harsh fluorescent lighting and stained linoleum floor, she looked around. It was a moment before she realized she was looking for Josie. Which was funny because she generally made a point of avoiding Josie in school. She hadn't wanted to mix Josie and her friends, what with Josie knowing her secret. Josie's basement-level social status didn't help, either.

But right now Gabby couldn't make herself care about that. She trusted Josie to keep her secret and knew how much Josie was hurting over the loss of Clementine. Gabby wasn't sure what she'd do if she found Josie—would she actually walk over to her and say something?

After a minute, she realized Josie wasn't there, anyway. Which was probably for the best—it was safest just to keep her hospital work in its own package, separate from school.

AFTER SCHOOL, GABBY walked briskly through the gray afternoon, heading for the hospital. She was feeling good these days—Dr. Klein had her on new meds that were less draining than the last ones had been. And so far no signs of another seizure.

As she turned the corner of Buttercup Avenue, a block away from the hospital, she saw someone walking ahead of her, nearly swallowed up in a big blue down jacket.

"Josie," Gabby called, running so she could catch up to her.

Josie turned, and Gabby's breath snagged in her chest. Josie's eyes were dull and red-rimmed with dark circles underneath. Her normally pink cheeks were pale, and her face, usually so animated, was lifeless.

"You haven't found her yet," Gabby said more than asked.

Josie's eyes filled with tears, and she swiped at them. "My mom and I drove around last night and then this morning before school, but no sign of her." Even her voice was leaden.

"I'm so sorry," Gabby said. "Let me know if I can help you put up flyers or anything."

Josie's mouth moved in what was an attempt at a smile. "Thanks, but my mom and her work friends are taking care of it," she said. "Since they're out all over town delivering mail, they can put flyers up everywhere in just a couple of hours."

"Great," Gabby said as they walked into the hospital, the warmth and the sounds of carols playing softly in the lobby wrapping around them. "I bet someone will call." She actually wasn't so sure of this—she knew from cop shows that the longer someone was missing, the less likely it was that they would be found. Well, on the shows it was missing people, but she was pretty sure it was the same principle for lost dogs, too.

And by the way Josie's eyes filled with tears again, Gabby knew she felt the same.

"Let's not talk about it," Josie said. "I want to just try to forget about it for a couple of hours, you know?"

Gabby knew. "You've got it," she said. But as they took the elevator up to the second floor, she thought of something. "Everyone's going to ask you about it, though. Why don't you let me go ahead and ask Nurse Joe to tell people she's not back yet, and that you'd rather not talk about it."

"That would be great, if you don't mind," Josie said. This time, her smile came closer to the real thing.

So Josie waited in the area right outside the ward while Gabby gave Nurse Joe the heads-up.

"I'm on it," he said after she'd explained. "In two minutes, everyone will know not to say a word about Clementine."

"Thanks," Gabby said, heading back to get Josie.

When she turned the corner, she saw that Josie wasn't alone. She was standing with the woman from the X-ray department and two guys in lab coats. Gabby hurried over.

"This is Javier and Baxter," Josie said. "They want to do the skeleton Christmas skit for the Festival."

"Awesome!" Gabby bubbled.

"Yeah, we have some good ideas," Javier said, rubbing his palms gleefully.

Gabby laughed, and Josie made a sound that was almost a laugh. "I can't wait to see it," Gabby said.

The three X-ray techs walked toward the elevators, and Gabby turned to Josie, beaming. "You did it," she said happily. "You signed up a brand-new act for the Festival."

"Yeah," Josie said, smiling her first real smile of the afternoon.

Oscar was already in the lounge when they got there, though instead of sitting on the sofa, he was standing up and looking out the window. "I have to go early today," he said when they walked in, no hello or anything.

"No problem," Josie said.

Gabby waited for him to at least give Josie a sympathetic look, but he just gazed back out the window silently. Yet another moment of him being selfish, which irritated Gabby—Josie deserved better than that. But there was no point in bringing it up since it would just upset Josie, so Gabby moved on to something she knew would make Josie happy. "Let's talk about the Festival really quick before we go see the kids," she said, reaching into her pocket for her phone.

The one thing she could think of to cheer Josie up was to make the Festival happen. "We have seven acts so far, which is awesome."

Josie nodded. In the harsh light of the lounge, her eyes looked almost bruised. She clearly hadn't slept much, if at all, last night.

"For a full show, we just need two more acts," Gabby went on, keeping her voice cheery. "And then we need someone to lead the carol sing-along and we have to get started with the sibling act." She raised an eyebrow at Oscar, ready for another one of his lame excuses.

"Right, I had an idea for that," Oscar said. "'Frosty the Snowman.' The kids can act out the story and then sing at the end."

Gabby was impressed, despite herself. "That sounds good," she said.

"Totally," Josie agreed.

"Okay," Oscar said. "So maybe I'll go now and see which siblings want to sign up."

He was out the door before Gabby could offer to get him in touch with her brothers. Which she thought was kind of weird—what was the rush?

But Josie looked pleased. "I told you he'd come through," she said, not in a smug way, just happy it had worked out.

"I guess I was wrong about him," Gabby said. She actually wasn't so sure, but she was glad he was finally taking care of the act. It cleared the way for Gabby to pitch her new idea to Josie.

"I was thinking something, too, actually," she said, tucking a curl behind one ear. "I know you don't want to do a solo, but what about leading the carol sing-along? You could wear a costume and you'd be with a group of kids up onstage, so you wouldn't be alone or anything." This was a compromise for Gabby—she really wanted to see Josie do a solo and completely awe everyone. But she couldn't pressure Josie now, when she was so sad about Clementine. And maybe if Josie did the sing-along this year, it would give her the courage to perform by herself the next time.

Josie was biting her lip. "I'm not sure," she said. "I mean, there will be a lot of people there."

"Right, but you'll be all dressed up with a big crowd of kids around you," Gabby said.

"Let me think about it," Josie said.

Gabby sighed but didn't push—at least Josie hadn't said no. "Sure," she said. "And who else should we ask to perform?"

Josie considered for a moment, then shook her head. "We're running out of people to ask," she said, beginning to twist the sleeve of her sweater.

"We haven't asked administrators," Gabby said. "Or any of the orderlies and nurses who work in other wards."

"I think most of the nurses in the hospital who will be here are doing something," Josie said. "Either in Nurse Joe's skit or helping out backstage."

"What about orderlies and administrators?" Gabby suggested.

"We can ask them," Josie said. "Though right now we should probably get ready to go see the kids."

"Right," Gabby said. She liked how Josie just knew she was coming along without even asking.

They headed into the closet and selected their costumes, then headed out for an afternoon of performing.

A LITTLE BEFORE it was time to go, Gabby left Josie to sing in Melanie's room and went to the staff lounge. There was no way she could make Josie ask for Festival volunteers when she felt this bad, so Gabby was hoping to sign up another act herself. There were two orderlies there who both claimed stage fright but said they'd ask around. They also volunteered to help pass out programs at the show, so her trip down there wasn't a total loss. Still, they were getting down to the wire. Gabby made a quick detour to the administrative office, but it was closed for the day. A sliver of anxiety poked into her but she put on a smile when she got back to the peds ward and found Josie.

"We'll go to the administrators tomorrow," Gabby said after she'd updated Josie and they were heading to the volunteer room. "And maybe one of the other orderlies will want to do an act."

"I hope so," Josie said. She had perked up for their performances, but now she drooped a bit in her costume and was picking at her thumbnail. She was probably dreading going home without Clementine in addition to worrying about the Festival, and Gabby wished she could have brought back better news.

Oscar had joined them for a few songs and mentioned that he'd gotten some siblings to sign up, but he was already gone when they walked into the lounge. Which was annoying because Gabby wanted to get the names for her list and also give him her home phone number so he could invite her brothers. They were going to be very excited. But there was time for that tomorrow, too.

"Henry loved it when we sang 'Up on the Rooftop,'" Gabby said as she and Josie went into the costume closet.

"Yeah, but he missed Clementine," Josie said. Her eyes welled with tears as she said her dog's name.

"We all do," Gabby said, putting a hand on Josie's arm. Josie was wearing a candy cane–striped dress with none of her usual flourishes, which was almost as sad as the tears that slid down her cheeks.

"I broke my own rule about mentioning her," Josie said, rubbing the tears off her face. "Let's talk about something else."

"We can talk about whatever you want," Gabby said.

"Really?" Josie asked.

"Sure," Gabby said. She was distracted by how hard it was to pull off a curled elf shoe. Though it had been quite fun marching around the hospital in them.

"Why did you want to help us with the Festival?" Josie asked quietly.

The boot came off suddenly, causing Gabby to fall backward. She took a moment to regain her balance and figure out what to say.

But then she looked up at Josie, who had always

been honest with her. And she knew she owed Josie the truth.

"Remember how I asked you not to tell anyone about my epilepsy?" she asked, tugging absently on a curl.

Josie nodded.

"It's just—I couldn't trust that you'd keep my secret," Gabby said. "I didn't know you well then, and I thought you might want to tell people."

Josie was looking at her blankly.

"Some people like to spread gossip," Gabby clarified. "And I wasn't sure if you and Oscar were like that. So I figured if I was helping you, you'd, I don't know, feel obligated to help me back."

"So you wanted to help us so that we'd owe you," Josie said.

"It sounds awful when you say it like that," Gabby said. "But yeah. I really needed to keep it a secret."

"Why?" Josie asked.

Gabby bit her lip. She wasn't sure she could tell this story.

"It's just," Josie went on. "Epilepsy is no big deal, and it seems like it's probably stressful to keep it hidden."

So Josie was a mind reader.

"Um, maybe a little," Gabby said, spinning half-truths and veiled stories through her head to see which one would work best. But then she looked into Josie's warm brown eyes that were full of concern. And Gabby knew she could tell this story: She could tell it to Josie. "Everyone at my old school hated me because of it."

Josie's forehead wrinkled. "That's so weird," she said. "Because epilepsy is seriously no big thing. It's not like you had leprosy and big chunks of skin kept falling off you when you walked down the hall."

At that, Gabby giggled, something she would not have believed possible when discussing what had happened to her that year.

"So why did people freak out?" Josie asked. She was leaning back against the shoe shelves.

Gabby had never imagined she would say the words out loud to anybody, ever. But now, in the cozy costume room surrounded by piles of satin and velveteen and bright colors that smelled of mint and pine, with Josie listening so carefully, it turned out it was easy. "I had a seizure in front of my best friend and I wet my pants."

She waited for Josie to gasp and put a hand to her

chest, or race out of the room in disgust. But Josie did none of those things.

"So?" she asked. "I mean, that can happen during a seizure, but so what?"

Gabby fought an urge to throw her arms around Josie. "Jenny thought it was gross and she told everyone and then the whole school started calling me a bed wetter," Gabby said.

"That's so dumb," Josie said, a flash of fire in her tone. "Why do people do mean, stupid stuff like that?"

Gabby shrugged. "Jenny always liked spreading gossip," she said. "And I don't think she expected it to blow up as much as it did."

"She should have realized what immature jerks fourth-grade boys can be," Josie said.

Gabby snickered at that.

"Jenny was stupid and petty and I bet she regretted it after she did it," Josie went on.

That had certainly never occurred to Gabby. "Why?" she asked.

"Because she lost you as a friend," Josie said. "And you are a really good friend."

Josie thought they were friends. Real friends, the kind Gabby had sworn she'd never have again because of what had happened with Jenny. But Josie, in her candy-cane dress, with her indignation at Jenny and her staunch defense of Gabby—she *was* a friend. A good one. And even if Gabby wanted to, there was no backing away from that now.

And as Gabby grinned at Josie, she realized something. She didn't want to. She was ready to have a real friend in her life again.

Chapter 18

Thursday, December 15

Oscar had ducked out of Melanie's room while Josie and Gabby were singing "Up on the Rooftop." He was pretty sure they hadn't noticed him leave. They'd been having so much fun laughing together, they barely even noticed he was there, which was a good thing. Right now, Oscar didn't want either of them, especially Josie, noticing him.

The gray afternoon had turned into a glacial evening, the kind where just walking through the icy air made Oscar's face sting from the cold. He hurried down Buttercup Avenue, the lights of the hospital disappearing in the darkness behind him. He'd come to enjoy volunteering over the past weeks, but now that had changed, kind of how everything was changing.

Just thinking of his parents' separation was a sharp punch right in the center of his rib cage. Oscar drew in a shaky breath. The days since the announcement had been more bitter than the cold numbing his cheeks, and Oscar wasn't sure how he'd managed to get through them. Well, he was, actually. There was something that had helped, a lot, although it was kind of another whole mess he'd have to fix.

Oscar opened the door to his dark house and heard happy barking. A moment later, a little fur missile launched into his arms, covering his face with warm, sloppy dog kisses.

"Hey, Clementine," Oscar said, hugging her tight.

OSCAR HADN'T PLANNED to take Clementine, which he thought made the whole thing just a little bit better. The dog had followed him out of the hospital, and Oscar hadn't even noticed until they were several blocks away. At first he was going to turn right around and take Clementine back. But when she pressed herself against him, warm and snug, he remembered what he was going home to, how awful it all was. And he knew it would be just a little bit easier if Clementine was there.

"You can walk home with me," he'd told the dog, who yipped as though she understood. "And then we'll call Josie."

So together they walked through the snow to Oscar's house.

His mom had been surprised when she got home and discovered Clementine.

"She belongs to a friend," Oscar had said. "Can we watch her for a little?" He was starting to realize there was no way he could give Clementine back that night. It just felt too good having her there. He'd tell Josie the next day at school instead. It would probably be easier for her to pick up the dog then, anyway.

"Sure," his mom had said. "A little furry company would do us some good, I think."

And so it had.

That night Oscar had lain in bed hearing his parents' past arguments echoing in the dark. He remembered the time the family took a trip to Lake Placid, and his mom, who was driving, messed up the directions and got them lost. His dad couldn't stop stewing about how anyone could possibly get lost when they were using a GPS, his mom exploded, and they were barely speaking when the family finally arrived. Then there was the time his dad forgot to come to his last baseball game of the season. His mom had muttered about that for weeks, long after Oscar himself had gotten over it. The worst arguments were always at Christmas, though. Last year, when his parents fought over whether to get a real or artificial tree. The year before, when they stopped speaking for days because they disagreed on how much to spend on presents. And the year before that, on Christmas Day, when his dad, who had been working late for weeks, forgot to get something for his mom and wrapped up a homemade gift certificate for something lame. Oscar couldn't remember what the certificate was for exactly, only that it had been so weak, his mom had been infuriated, saying that if he cared about her at all, he'd have found five minutes to get her something decent. Maybe if they'd just skipped Christmas every year, his parents would still be together. Which made Oscar hate Christmas almost as much as he hated the fact that his family was breaking into messy pieces, like a vase shattered on the floor. And who knew what would become of the shards?

That was what sat like a ball of wet cement in his stomach, and the only thing that helped was the fuzzy dog next to him, cuddled up close and licking the tears off his face.

So one night had turned into two, and Oscar was no closer to returning Clementine to Josie. Which was awful, Oscar knew; he really did.

But the thought of facing his father's stony gaze or the sound of his mother crying when she thought Oscar was asleep—how could he live through those things without Clementine?

"Tomorrow," Oscar told the cuddly dog, finally releasing her and heading for the kitchen to give her dinner. "I'll take you back tomorrow."

Chapter 19

"I brought you something," Josie said to Oscar. She'd waited for him in front of the school and ran to meet him when she saw him trudging up the path through the snow.

"I hope you like blueberry muffins," Josie said, handing him the bag of fresh muffins that her grandma had gotten up early to bake for Josie. Her family had been doing all they could to help ease the pain of losing Clementine. Josie had thanked her grandma, but ever since her beloved dog had disappeared, Josie had barely been able to choke down food at all. Still, she knew someone who could use the muffins, someone who was having a hard time, just like she was. So she'd packed them up for Oscar.

The bag was moist and warm, steam spilling out when Oscar opened it.

"Thanks," he said, not quite looking at her and not taking a muffin as they walked up the recently cleared steps of the school. He'd been distant like this for days, and Josie ached for her friend who was going through so much.

"Go ahead and eat one," Josie said. "They're good."

They'd arrived inside the lobby and were being jostled on all sides.

"Later," Oscar said. He slipped through the crowd and was gone.

• • • 🦴 • • •

THAT AFTERNOON, JOSIE headed home before going to the hospital. Her mom was only working a half day today, and she had promised to drive Josie around town to look for Clementine yet again. Josie could tell by the looks her mom exchanged with her grandparents that they all thought it was hopeless. But Josie couldn't give up on her Clementine, not yet.

"Hi, Mom," Josie said, walking through the front door.

"Hi, sweetie," her mom said, coming down the stairs. She smiled at Josie, but Josie saw the tightness around her mouth and braced herself. What if there was bad news about Clementine?

"I hate to ask you about this now, hon, but I got a call from the real estate agent about that apartment," her mom said. "They need to know pretty soon if I want it. They said they'd give us until right after Christmas, but I wondered what you were thinking about it."

Josie hadn't been thinking about anything except Clementine. The idea of agreeing to an apartment where Clementine wouldn't be able to live if—*when*—they found her was unthinkable. But so was crushing her mom's dream of living independently.

Josie opened her mouth, not knowing what to say, but just then the doorbell rang. Josie turned and opened the door. And then she blinked because she couldn't be seeing what she thought she was seeing.

Clementine flew into her arms, furry, snowy, and wriggling with joy. Josie burst into tears as she sat down right there in the doorway so she could hug Clementine, possibly never letting her go.

"Hey," someone said. Josie looked up to see Oscar standing there, shifting his weight from side to side.

"You found Clementine." Josie gulped as she tried to make the tears stop. Clementine, ever helpful, began to lick her cheeks, which tickled and made Josie giggle.

"Kind of," Oscar said, now staring at a point in the distance.

"Thank you," Josie's mom said. She had come to the door and was smiling down at Clementine, who gave a happy bark. Josie's mom patted the dog's head, then went back inside.

Josie stood up and hugged Oscar. "Yes, thank you," she said. "I was so worried and I just—thank you." It wasn't enough. She wanted to bake Oscar cookies and write poems about him and announce to the world that he was a hero.

Oscar kept his arms at his sides, his body rigid. Obviously, he wasn't a hugger.

But then he cleared his throat. "Actually, it's my fault she was gone," he said.

Josie took a step back. "What?" she asked.

"She followed me out of the hospital that night she went missing," Oscar said, the words coming out in a rush. "I knew I should have called you, but I—I needed her."

And now Josie wanted to bake him poison cookies and write horrible poems about him and tell the world he was a thief and a liar and a total fraud as a friend.

"My parents are splitting up," Oscar said, his voice cracking on the last word. "And having her with me helped so much and I just—I couldn't tell you about it."

He seemed to think Josie would be okay with this, that she would understand, but he was quite mistaken.

"Why?" she asked, the word sharp in the icy air. "Why couldn't you tell me?" Clementine pressed herself against Josie's legs, and Josie buried her fingers in Clementine's downy fur.

"I needed her," Oscar said, like that was all that mattered.

"I need her, too," Josie said. "You saw how hard this was for me, and you just let me go on not knowing if my dog was okay or if she was even still alive." Her voice broke.

"I'm sorry," Oscar said, looking down at the gloves he was twisting in his hands.

"If you'd told me it helped to have her, I would have let you keep her as long as you needed," Josie said. "All you had to do was ask."

It looked as though asking had never occurred to Oscar. And Josie realized why: Oscar was not an asker; he was a taker. Gabby had seen it all along: the way Oscar shrugged off hard work, the way he had to be pushed to help out with one tiny part of the Festival that meant so much to Josie. The way he just gave her a stupid nod at school, as though to say hi would embarrass him.

"I brought you muffins," Josie said, unable to believe she'd done something thoughtful for the boy who had stolen her dog and stabbed her in the back.

"Yeah, that's why I brought her back," Oscar said. "You've been nice to me and—"

"And you have not been nice to me." Josie bit off the words.

"Josie, I'm sorry, really," Oscar pleaded.

Josie was having none of it. She ushered her dog in and slammed the door behind them.

Then she slid down to the floor, wrapping her arms around her dog. Josie was furious with Oscar, but in this moment, nothing mattered more than Clementine, wriggly and warm and utterly perfect. "I missed you," Josie said, pressing her face against the dog's warm middle. "So, so much."

Clementine gave a soft bark, as if to say she had missed Josie, too.

"How wonderful that that boy brought Clementine home," Josie's mom said, coming in and crouching down so she could scratch Clementine's ears.

And then Josie remembered the conversation her mom had started, right before Oscar the betrayer had brought her dog home. As Clementine licked her cheek, Josie knew she had her answer for her mom.

"Mom, I can't give Clementine up," she said. "I can't. I'm sorry, but it was just so awful when she was gone and—" Josie stopped and took a ragged breath, not able to finish.

"I understand," her mom said quietly. She smiled at Josie. Her eyes were so sad, Josie's insides felt squashed, as if something was squeezing them tight and not letting go.

But as Clementine began wagging her short tail, her mouth open in her doggy half smile, Josie knew she had made the only choice she could.

Chapter 20

Saturday, December 17

"We really need to find two more acts today," Gabby said as soon as she arrived at the volunteer room on Saturday morning. "Like now. We only have three days left to rehearse and get everything set for the Festival." It was only then that she noticed Oscar sitting on the chair, looking as though he'd learned he was being exiled to Siberia, and Josie standing near the costume closet, arms crossed over her chest. What was going on with them?

Before she could ask, a fuzzy tan dog bounded over to her and yipped a happy greeting.

"Clementine," Gabby gasped. She bent down to hug the little dog just as the door behind them pushed open and Ms. D'Amato walked in.

"Did I hear someone talking about the Festival?" Ms. D'Amato asked. "Because I have a surprise for you."

"Great," Gabby said, trying to focus. But she

couldn't help feeling disoriented. Clementine was back, so why did Josie and Oscar look so upset?

"I'm going to be one of your acts," Ms. D'Amato said, grinning.

"Awesome," Gabby said, thrilled to hear it. Even Josie was smiling.

"I'm not a performer, but my sister's a bit of a ham, so we're going to do a song and dance routine with a few of our friends," Ms. D'Amato said. "We're making up a silly version of 'Twelve Days of Christmas.'"

"That sounds fantastic," Josie said, and Gabby agreed completely.

"So does that give us enough acts?" Ms. D'Amato asked.

"We have nine including you," Gabby said. "But I know we'll find a tenth today."

Ms. D'Amato pressed her lips together for a moment. "Maybe we can just go ahead with nine," she said hesitantly. "I know how hard you guys have worked, and I'd hate to throw it all away over just one act."

"Would only nine acts be okay?" Josie asked.

Ms. D'Amato sighed. "What's tough is that it's a lot of work to move some of the kids out of their rooms, and so many people come from the community. We want to make sure we have a real show for them, and we've always had ten acts as the minimum. But I know you've done a lot of—"

"We'll get ten," Josie said firmly.

Gabby was shocked. Ms. D'Amato had just handed them a free pass, and Josie was turning it down.

"We want it to be the best Festival ever," Josie said, to both Ms. D'Amato and Gabby.

"Ten really would be ideal," Ms. D'Amato said. "But either way, have the names of the performers to me by the nineteenth so we can start printing up the programs."

"I thought we had until the twentieth," Gabby said quickly.

"The printer said they need it by the nineteenth," Ms. D'Amato said. "Will that be a problem? Maybe we can find another printer."

The poor volunteer coordinator looked exhausted at the thought.

Gabby was worried—they were running out of options and the nineteenth was only two days away. But she gave Ms. D'Amato her dazzling smile. "It's no problem," she said.

Ms. D'Amato headed out. As soon as the door swished closed behind her, Gabby turned to Oscar and Josie. "Let's do this," she said.

"Yes, but I'm not going with him," Josie said, the way she'd announce she wasn't going anywhere with a large rat. Clementine went over to Josie and pressed her furry self against Josie's legs, as though to soothe her.

"Wait, can we talk about how Clementine's back?" Gabby asked. She'd gotten so swept up in Festival plans, she'd nearly forgotten the fantastic turn of events.

"Yes, the person who stole her returned her," Josie said tartly.

"I didn't steal her," Oscar said, holding up his arms.

"Then what would you call it?" Josie asked, her voice laced with sarcasm. "Borrowing? I don't think so because borrowing involves asking and you didn't ask."

Gabby was light-headed from all of this. "Wait, *Oscar* took Clementine?"

"She followed me home," Oscar said, pleading with Gabby to understand.

"And you never bothered to tell Josie?" Gabby asked, hearing her voice rise but not caring. How could Oscar have done that?

Her words seemed to take something out of him, and he slouched down. "Yeah," he said quietly. "I took

Clementine. I stole her. And I'm sorry. I really am."
He sounded defeated, and Gabby was surprised to
feel a sliver of sympathy for him.

"I'm glad you can admit you stole her," Josie said.
"I'm going to find a final act for the Festival now."
And with that, she grabbed Clementine's leash and
stalked out of the lounge.

Gabby followed, feeling as though she was going
after a stranger. Where had this angry, outspoken
Josie come from?

"I'm so glad you have Clementine back," Gabby
said when she caught up with Josie.

"Yeah, me too," Josie said. "And you were right
about Oscar. He's a total backstabbing jerk."

Gabby wasn't sure she'd ever actually said that.
And she couldn't help thinking about the sorrow in
Oscar's face. "It seems like he does feel sorry," she said.

"Whatever, I don't care," Josie said. "He wasn't
ever a real friend, not like you are."

Gabby considered this for a moment.

"Josie, Gabby," Nurse Joe called just as they'd
reached the elevators. "I'm glad I caught you guys. I
have some rough news: Rosie's back."

Josie drew in a sharp breath, but Gabby wasn't
sure who he was talking about.

"Rosie's five," Nurse Joe explained, noticing her confusion the way he noticed everything. "She has cerebral palsy, and she was in recently for surgery. It actually went well, but she's back now with an infection."

"Is she up for visitors?" Josie asked.

"I think a short one would do her a world of good," Nurse Joe said.

"We're on our way," Gabby said. The Festival was important, but this mattered more.

The girls started back down the hall.

"Hey, where's Santa's Secret Agent?" Nurse Joe asked.

Gabby saw Josie's whole body stiffen. "We were just going to see about signing up another act for the Festival," she said, even though it didn't really answer the question.

Nurse Joe's forehead creased, but he didn't say anything as they started for Rosie's room.

Rosie's dad was dozing in the chair next to Rosie. Her cheeks were a mottled, unnatural pink, and her hair was matted and sweaty. But her eyes lit up when she saw them. "Daddy, look who's here," she said. Her voice was scratchy, and her words were a bit slurred.

"And this is my friend Gabby," Josie said, her voice gentle. "Are you up for a song?"

Rosie nodded, then winced as if the movement had hurt.

Rosie's dad, who had dark circles under his eyes, nodded, too. "A short one," he said. "Rosie is in some pain, and she needs to rest while the medicine kicks in."

Gabby's heart twisted. Rosie was so small; she should be out ice-skating with friends, not stuck in a hospital room, hurting. But Rosie smiled eagerly, and Gabby saw how much one song meant to her.

"Is 'Little Drummer Boy' okay?" Josie asked Gabby.

Gabby nodded and they began. As usual, Gabby was mesmerized by how rich and pure Josie's voice sounded as it rang out in the small room. It was just wrong that she refused to sing in the Festival.

Rosie sighed happily when they were done, then leaned back against her pillow and closed her eyes.

"Thanks," her dad said. His face moved into a shadow of a smile. "She loves it when you visit—these shows really lift her spirits."

"We'll come back again tomorrow, then," Josie said, and Gabby nodded.

"Great," Rosie's dad said.

They tiptoed out, not wanting to disturb Rosie as she fell asleep.

"Poor thing," Gabby said when they were back in the hall.

"Yeah, she's really going through a lot," Josie said.

They were silent for a moment, then Josie glanced at the clock on the wall. "We should get to the administrators' office before they all go home," she said. "Then we can come back and sing for the other kids since Oscar probably bailed on us."

They headed to the elevators, and Josie led the way to a large room on the first floor. Gabby focused on the task at hand as they walked into the room with its beige walls and landscapes. There were no holiday decorations, which kind of seemed like a bad sign, but there was a bowl of mints on the counter. Good thing Oscar wasn't there to tip them over. Gabby was surprised to realize she actually kind of missed having him around, though.

"No dogs allowed," the woman behind the desk said. She was tall, even sitting, and her black hair was tied in a bun without a single strand out of place.

"Oh, sorry," Josie said, backing out and taking Clementine with her.

"I'm allergic," the woman said to Gabby. She was reaching for a tissue, despite the fact that Clementine had been in the room less than ten seconds. "What can I do for you girls?"

Gabby explained about the Festival.

"Yes, we all love going to that," the woman said. "But I'm not sure any of us can help. I don't like to perform, and I know Katya is very shy. I can't imagine she'd agree to anything. And the others will be away on the twenty-fourth."

"Thanks, anyway," Gabby said, knowing this was a dead end.

"What did she say?" Josie asked when Gabby walked back into the hall.

"It was a negative," Gabby said. A new idea was starting to take shape as she looked at this strong, determined Josie who wasn't willing to settle for a substandard show.

"Uh-oh," Josie said. "We're really getting down to the wire. Who else do you think we can ask?"

"Um, maybe we can think about it while we perform for the kids," Gabby said. Her idea was beginning to take hold, and the more she thought about it, the more she was convinced it was the best idea ever.

Chapter 21

Saturday, December 17

J osie refused to perform with him, so Oscar was left on his own to wander through the kids' rooms on the peds ward. By now he knew everyone pretty well, and since Josie and Gabby were singing up a storm, Oscar mostly just chatted with the kids. Which was fine, obviously, because it was easy. Sure he'd come to kind of enjoy singing, but it wasn't like he missed it. Much.

"Hey, Secret Agent," Jade said as she and Ed passed. They were dressed as candy canes, and Jade was wearing tap shoes that clinked when she walked.

"Hey," Oscar said, thankful that at least some people were talking to him.

He was heading over to Alison, who'd come in for physical therapy, when he felt an iron grip on his elbow.

"We need to talk," Gabby said, steering him into the lounge, her black boots tapping and red plush skirt swinging. He'd been taken hostage by Mrs. Claus. She didn't let go of his arm until they were sitting on the sofa.

"You need to make things right with Josie, and I know how you can do it," Gabby announced, taking charge like she always did and smoothing the skirt of her Mrs. Claus costume. "But first I need to know if it's worth it to ask you because I'm still trying to figure out if you're a jerk or not."

Like he was going to have a conversation about that. But when he tried to get up, Gabby grabbed him in her vice-like grip again. "Why did you take Clementine?" she asked.

He debated wrenching his arm free, but what was the point? She'd probably just follow him, and what was happening to his family wasn't going to be a secret much longer.

"My parents are splitting up," he said, fiddling with his Secret Agent sunglasses. "And when Clementine followed me, it was easier to be home with her there." He hadn't expected to say so much, but she was nodding.

"I'm sorry about your parents," Gabby said. "You know, my aunt and uncle split up two years ago, and it was really tough for my cousins at first. But now their parents are a lot happier, and they are, too."

This was not helpful—nothing was going to be better about his family being blown apart. "Maybe," he said shortly. "Anyway, that's why I took the dog."

Gabby pulled on a curl. "I shouldn't tell you it's going to get better," she said after a moment. "I don't know what it's like for you. But I do know what it's like when everything's awful and that's really hard." She looked at Oscar. "I get why you kept Clementine. I'm not saying it was okay, but I get it."

Something unclenched inside Oscar at her words, and he grinned. "Does this mean I pass your test?"

Gabby laughed. "Yes, good news for you, you're not a complete jerk."

"I'm so glad it's official," Oscar said, rolling his eyes.

"And it means I think you can work things out with Josie," Gabby went on. She'd taken off her plush hat and was folding it up absently as she spoke.

At that, Oscar stopped smiling. "She really hates me," he said. Thinking about it made him feel like he had last winter on Sutter Hill when he'd fallen off his sled and gotten the wind knocked out of him.

But now Gabby was the one rolling her eyes. "Josie likes you," she said. "That's why she's acting like she hates you."

Oscar's brows scrunched together. "That doesn't make sense."

"Of course it does," Gabby said impatiently, like Oscar was the unreasonable one. "It means you hurt her feelings. If she really didn't care, she wouldn't make such a big point of showing you."

That made even less sense.

"Okay, forget it, I can see that part's too complicated," Gabby said. "The point is, I have an idea for how you can make it up to her."

Oscar still didn't believe it was true, but if it was . . . "I'm listening," he said.

"It starts with a flashy apology," Gabby said. Oscar had no idea what that would even be. "You're going to have to figure that out because it has to be true to you."

That didn't exactly help, but before he could ask, Gabby went on. "The big thing is that you're going to persuade her to sing a solo in the show."

"But she doesn't want to," Oscar pointed out. Pressuring Josie to sing seemed like a good way to make her hate him more, not less.

"I think she does want to, though," Gabby said. "She's just scared."

"If she's scared, maybe it's not a good idea," Oscar pointed out. He was starting to think Gabby's great plan was a complete bust.

Gabby glared at him. "You can't let fear make your

choices," she said. Then she drew in a breath, like she had just thought about what she'd said. "I guess we all do that, but we shouldn't, and in this case, Josie really shouldn't. She's an amazing singer, and it's time she stood in the spotlight."

"Maybe," Oscar said. It was actually a pretty good point. And Oscar had a feeling Gabby was right—somewhere, hidden away, Josie really did want to find the courage to sing. "But what makes you think I'm the one to persuade her?"

"Here's the thing," Gabby said in a way that told Oscar he was not going to like "the thing" at all. "You've been a selfish friend to Josie."

Oscar opened his mouth to argue, but Gabby held up a hand.

"Can you honestly deny it?" she asked. "You don't hang out with her at school, you let her do all the work at the hospital, and if that wasn't enough, you stole her dog. I get why you did it, but still, dog theft is low on the list of good friend qualities."

"How do you know I don't hang out with her at school?" Oscar asked. "You're too busy being popular to notice what anyone else is doing."

"*Do* you sit with her at lunch?" Gabby asked, eyes flashing again. "Or walk with her in the halls or talk to her by her locker?"

Oscar wilted. "No," he said. "But I bet you don't, either." That was pretty much the last of his fight because he knew Gabby was right, on all counts. He *had* been a pretty crummy friend to Josie. And when he thought about how she'd listened to him about his parents, the way she understood what he was saying—and the way she'd thought to bring him muffins—he felt lower than the crud on the bottom of his sneakers.

"You're right. I haven't been hanging out with Josie in school," Gabby retorted. "But that's changing, starting on Monday." She looked at him with a raised eyebrow. "We're not talking about me right now, anyway, we're talking about you. And you know what I'm saying is true."

"Yeah," he said begrudgingly.

Gabby smiled and unfolded the hat. "So if you want to show Josie that you're thinking about something besides yourself for a change, make a big apology and tell her she needs to get over her stage fright and sing that solo already."

Oscar still wasn't sure about any of this. "What's a big apology?" he asked, figuring that was the more important thing. If Josie didn't accept his apology, she wouldn't listen to anything he said about performing. "Like say it loudly or writing it down?"

Gabby rolled her eyes. "No, it's just both saying and showing you're sorry."

That did not clarify things at all.

"Start by thinking of who Josie is, what she cares about, what she loves," Gabby said. "And then figure out a way to use that to show her how sorry you are."

Oscar considered this. His dad once brought his mom chocolates to say he was sorry for missing their anniversary—maybe Oscar could get Josie food. After all, everyone liked to eat. But then he realized that wasn't exactly what Gabby had said: She'd said to think of Josie and what she liked, not just something anyone would like. Which might have been what went wrong with his dad's apology because now Oscar remembered that his mom had been on a no-sugar diet that month and had thrown the chocolate out.

Josie might reject his apology, too, but he could try. He owed her that. "I'll think about it," he said to Gabby.

"Okay, but think fast," Gabby said. "Because once she forgives you, you're going to have to work quickly to persuade her to sing that solo."

"I don't think it's going to be as easy as that," Oscar said. Honestly, it seemed pretty impossible.

"You're right," Gabby agreed, putting on the hat. "That's why we're going to put on a bit of pressure. I'm going to make sure we don't find a final act for the show."

"That's devious," Oscar said.

Gabby grinned. "It's being a good friend," she said. "You know how much she wants this Festival to happen. And for it to be the best ever."

"I guess you have it all figured out," Oscar said. He was kind of in awe. Gabby was the real secret agent around here.

Gabby stood up. "I do," she said. "And now it's up to you to pull it off."

Chapter 22

Monday, December 19

On Monday afternoon, Josie was walking down the hall after the final bell rang when she saw that Gabby was waiting at her locker.

Josie was nearly as shocked as she had been at lunch, when Gabby had found her in the library and dragged her to the cafeteria. Josie wasn't sure who was more stunned, her or Gabby's friends. Josie hadn't said much, but it had been fun to sit with people while she ate a sandwich she'd brought from home. And Gabby's friends were nice, though they seemed surprised when Gabby voiced some of her stronger opinions. Maybe they didn't know her quite as well as Josie did, though. That thought made Josie smile as she opened up her locker and began piling books into her backpack.

"We have to get to the hospital and find that last act for the Festival," Josie said, zipping up the bag.

"We only have"—she glanced at the clock on the wall—"an hour and seventeen minutes."

"Right," Gabby said, not sounding as urgent as she should have. "Maybe we can . . ."

Her words trailed off because there was a commotion farther down the hall. Kids who had been pushing to leave were now standing still, looking at something, or someone, coming down the hall. Some were laughing, and Josie saw two girls sneak out cell phones to take pictures. Whatever it was, it was big.

And then the crowd parted.

"Wait, that can't be," Gabby said, her hands coming up to her face.

But it was. Walking toward them was Oscar decked out in a full Grinch costume. He had on the green Grinch boots with their pointed toes, the fuzzy Grinch outfit, Grinchy gloves, and the Santa hat that the Grinch wears at the end of the book.

Josie's coat and scarf slipped out of her hands.

"Just for the record, this does not change my anti-Christmas stance," Oscar said as he walked up to them. "But the Grinch is your favorite, right?"

He'd remembered. Josie could only nod, still speechless.

"Okay, good, because it would mess things up if I put on the wrong costume," Oscar said.

Josie was still trying to wrap her mind around the fact that Oscar, boy of the single nod, was wearing a costume in school when he threw out his arms with flourish. "This is how I'm apologizing," he said. "I'm sorry I didn't tell you about Clementine. I should have."

That seemed to be the end of his speech. It hadn't been much, but then again, the costume kind of said it all.

Josie glanced at Gabby. Her cheeks were pink with the effort of fighting back a fit of laughter.

Then she looked back at Oscar. He stood in front of her waiting for her response, not caring about all the kids staring and laughing and taking pictures of him in his ridiculous costume.

"Okay," Josie said, starting to grin. "I forgive you."

"Good," Oscar said. "Because these Grinch shoes are really killing me."

IT WASN'T THAT hard to get Oscar back into the Grinch costume when they reached the hospital, though Josie didn't understand why he and Gabby were taking so long getting ready when they had less than an hour to find a last act. She'd even insisted they skip getting Clementine today so that they'd have enough time to ask people.

"Okay, I'm thinking we should go to the blood lab," Josie said when they were finally set. She and Gabby were both dressed as Whos, the townspeople from *The Grinch*. "Maybe someone there is willing to be in the Festival."

Gabby and Oscar exchanged a look.

"Actually, we should go to Rosie's room first," Oscar said. "While you guys were changing in the closet, I, uh, saw Ed and Jade who said Rosie was asking for you."

Josie was torn, but if Rosie needed her . . . "Okay," she said. "But then we really have to find that last act."

She couldn't understand why they were so calm when it felt like the entire fate of the Festival depended on finding a last performer. But she headed out into the hall and down to Rosie's room.

"How are you feeling today?" Josie asked as they walked in.

"Okay," Rosie said. The bottom half of her body was encased in a cast, but her eyes sparkled.

"The infection's been treated, so Rosie will be able to go home in a few days," her mom said.

"Great," Gabby said with a grin.

"Can we sing a Christmas carol for you?" Josie asked.

"Mommy likes the one about angels who stand up high," Rosie said, looking at Oscar for some reason.

"It's my mom's favorite, too," Josie said. She loved the peaceful look her mom got whenever she heard it.

"I don't know that one," Oscar said.

"Me neither," Gabby said, though Josie thought she remembered Gabby singing it with her once before.

Josie was about to suggest they choose something else, but then she saw Rosie looking proudly at her mom. Rosie wanted this to make her mom happy, and that made Josie's heart squeeze up in her chest. And so she opened her mouth and sang, her body vibrant and tingly as her voice soared.

"That was amazing," Rosie's mom said when Josie had finished, looking at her with an expression almost like wonder.

"Thanks," Josie said, clearing her throat as her cheeks warmed. "Um, we should go now, but we'll come see you again tomorrow."

"And at the festivus," Rosie said.

Josie stopped. "You mean the Festival? That's not for a few more days."

"But you're singing the angel song there, too, right?" Rosie asked.

"Actually, there are a lot of great acts," Josie fumbled. Was this something Gabby and Oscar had cooked up? "Funny skits and nurses singing together and everything. It's going to be great. And I can sing you the angel song right here."

But the corners of Rosie's mouth turned down. "You're not singing the angel song in the festivus?"

Josie was speechless, but Gabby stepped in. "We're still figuring it all out," she said as she guided Josie out, Oscar on their heels.

"You guys, I am not—" Josie began, but Oscar interrupted.

"I wanted Rosie to tell you, but it's what we think, too," he said, gesturing to Gabby, like they had suddenly become some kind of awful team united against her. "You should do this."

"There's no way," Josie said. But she knew she didn't sound quite as firm as she'd intended.

"Josie, your voice is gorgeous, and it's meant to be shared," Gabby said.

"I'm doing the sing-along," Josie said stubbornly, moving out of the way as an orderly pushed a tray of medication boxes down the hall. "I can't do both."

"Gabby's going to take over the sibling act," Oscar said. "And I'll do the sing-along. With a costume and everything."

Josie nearly fell over at that. "But you hate Christmas," she said.

"I'll do it, anyway," Oscar said.

Which meant he'd do it for her so she could sing a solo.

"We don't really need ten acts," she said slowly.

"But it would be better if we had ten," Gabby said gently. It was exactly what Josie had said, and she knew it was true. She also knew it was unlikely they'd find another act this late. Which meant it was up to her to make the Festival as awesome as they wanted it to be.

She was wavering.

"You can bring Clementine up onstage with you," Oscar added. "That way you won't be alone."

"And we'll be cheering for you from the sidelines," Gabby added. That was what Josie's dad had said, all those years ago when Josie was about to climb onto the stage for the sing-along at her very first Festival. He said he'd be cheering for her. And she knew that if she sang that solo now, her dad would be cheering for her again, thrilled to see her up on that stage once more.

Josie could see Ms. D'Amato heading down the hall toward them.

She looked at Oscar, who had worn a Grinch costume to school, and Gabby, who was outspoken and willing to help, even after what had happened to her at her last school. They weren't hiding, and maybe it was time for Josie to stop hiding, too—to be the girl her friends and her dad had always believed her to be.

"Okay," she said finally. "I'll try."

At that, Gabby and Oscar whooped and high-fived. They had become a team, Josie realized, but they were *her* team.

And then Gabby got serious. "Our first dress rehearsal is tomorrow, four o'clock sharp."

"If there's a dress rehearsal, does that mean we have a show list ready to go?" Ms. D'Amato asked with a big smile.

"Yes," Gabby said, pulling a piece of paper out of a pocket in her costume. "And here it is." She smiled what Josie had come to see was her real smile—not dazzling but big, a little bit goofy, and utterly beautiful.

"Wait, don't we have to add that I'm singing?" Josie asked as Gabby passed the paper over to Ms. D'Amato.

Gabby's smile got even bigger. "I've had you on that list for days," she said.

• • • 🦴 • • •

"SO THE FESTIVAL'S all set," Josie's mom said. The two of them were sitting on the sofa in front of their Christmas tree, the room lit only by the glowing white lights wrapped around its branches. "And now you just have the two dress rehearsals, right?"

"Yeah, though each act has been finding time to practice individually. When we have the dress rehearsal, it's just seeing how it all fits together," Josie said, reaching for a gingerbread man. After dinner, she and her mom had baked a batch of Christmas cookies, some of which they were going to give their neighbors, and the rest they were eating now.

"Well, I can't wait to see it," her mom said, leaning back with a happy sigh.

"Will you braid my hair for it?" Josie asked.

"Of course," her mom said, giving her a squeeze.

"Thanks," Josie said. "And guess what?" She'd planned to surprise her mom, but now she realized she wanted to tell her beforehand, when it was just the two of them. "I'm going to sing a solo."

Josie's mom put an arm around her shoulder and squeezed tight. "You're so brave," she said.

Josie leaned against her mom, wanting to tell her that the thought of performing in front of such a big group was utterly terrifying but just the tiniest bit exciting, too. She wanted to tell her mom that she'd never have found the courage to do it if it weren't for her new friends. And she wanted to tell her mom that knowing she would be there, watching, meant everything to Josie.

But the word *brave* stopped her. Because not so long ago Josie's mom had wanted to be brave. She had wanted to stand on her own two feet and make a new home for herself and for Josie. And Josie had said no.

Josie looked down at Clementine, curled at their feet, fast asleep. She had needed her dog so badly when her dad died. But five years had passed, and now Josie had new friends and a whole new life. A life where she was brave enough to sing in front of hundreds of people—just Josie, no mask, no costume. And maybe Clementine, who had always had a knack for knowing where she was most needed, had already realized this.

Which meant it was time for Josie to be brave here, too.

Josie took a deep, shaky breath. "Mom, do you think that apartment is still available?"

Chapter 23

Tuesday, December 20

"Gabby, is it true you dropped yearbook?" Becky asked, a little breathless as though she had run to their table in the cafeteria.

"Yeah," Gabby said, stirring her bowl of minestrone soup, today's lunch special. She had already dumped in two packages of crackers.

"It's not going to be the same without you," Becky said, deflating like a balloon with a small pinprick.

"It was kind of boring," Gabby pointed out. "The eighth graders have all the good jobs."

"I guess," Becky said, the corners of her mouth turning down a bit. "Maybe I should drop it, too."

"If you like it, you should keep doing it," Gabby said. She sipped a spoonful of soup. It was bland but warm, which was always good on an icy-cold day. Snow was falling outside the big windows, and the cars in the parking lot were slowly getting covered, turning into soft white drifts.

"So what are you doing after school these days, Gabby?" Aisha asked. "Because you don't seem to be around."

Gabby had known that sooner or later this question would come, and she was prepared. She wasn't ready to share all her secrets just yet, but it was time for this one to come out in the open. "I'm volunteering at the hospital," she said. "In the pediatric ward."

It felt good to say it out loud. She noticed Becky wrinkle her nose and exchange a glance with Aisha, but it didn't bother Gabby the way it would have a few weeks ago.

"Aren't you worried about catching something?" Aisha asked.

Gabby laughed. "No," she said. "They don't let volunteers into rooms with contagious diseases."

"What do you do there?" Isabelle asked.

"I work with Josie and Oscar putting on skits and singing for the kids."

"Wait, Oscar Madison?" Becky asked. "Isn't he like a juvenile delinquent?"

Gabby sat up straight. "No, he's not. I mean, he got in that one fight, but now he hangs out in the hospital cheering up sick kids, which I think is pretty awesome."

Becky shrank down in her seat.

"It was great when he showed up in a Grinch costume," Jasmine said, standing up. "This sandwich is gross." She'd gotten turkey—something Gabby had learned long ago was a mistake. "I need to go get something edible. Anyone want anything?"

"No, thanks," Gabby said, smiling at her. She liked Jasmine. Isabelle, too. Gabby had spent so much time getting people to like her that she hadn't even considered who she herself liked. And who she might want to hang out with instead of who she should hang out with. But she was starting to figure it out now. And there was one person she was very sure about, a person who was walking into the cafeteria.

"Josie, over here!" Gabby called, waving and not caring who saw.

Josie waved, nearly dropping her lunch bag.

"Who brings a lunch bag in sixth grade?" Aisha muttered to Becky.

"People who want decent food," Gabby snapped.

"Hey," Josie said, coming up in her baggy wool sweater and jeans that didn't fit quite right.

Aisha and Becky shared another look, and Gabby stood up. "This table is kind of crowded," she said to Josie. "Let's go sit over there." The only empty tables left were near the garbage, the ones where people with zero social status sat.

"Okay," Josie said, perfectly happy to sit anywhere with a friend.

Which was exactly how Gabby felt, too. She gathered up her stuff and led the way.

"I guess your friends don't want me at their table anymore," Josie said. She was opening her bag and not looking at Gabby.

"They're not my friends," Gabby said. "Not all of them, anyway. And I'm the one who needed a change of scenery."

"Are you sure?" Josie asked, now looking right at Gabby. Gabby knew that Josie was asking about more than the table. She was asking if Gabby was really okay giving up being the girl everyone liked. If Gabby was finally willing to step from behind the facade she'd worked for a year and a half to build and polish to a golden perfection. If Gabby was finally ready to be herself.

"Yeah," Gabby said with a grin. "I'm sure."

Chapter 24

Friday, December 23

"Oscar's here!" Henry shouted when Oscar walked into the auditorium for the final dress rehearsal. Henry and the other kids were there to practice the sing-along. They were gathered on one side of the huge stage with its red velvet curtains and endless rows of plush green seats. It really was just like a fancy theater in New York, or at least how Oscar imagined one of those theaters would be.

"Hi, Oscar!" Freddy yelled. He was with his older brother, who was going to be in the sibling act, and he saluted Oscar as though he was a five-star general.

"Santa's Secret Agent!" Rosie cheered from where she rested on a stretcher, even though today Oscar was decked out in the elf costume he would wear for the sing-along.

"Oscar, come on," Alison called. "We've been waiting for you!"

Oscar grinned and waved. "Hey, everybody," he said.

He was about to walk over to join them when he felt a hand come down on his shoulder. He turned and was shocked to see Ms. Antonoff.

"Mr. Madison," the principal said. "I see you've got quite the fan club."

Oscar felt his cheeks warm, but he wasn't sure what to say.

"I'm on the hospital's outreach committee, and we've been invited to observe your rehearsal," she said. Families of performers were invited, too, to give everyone a sense of performing in front of an audience. Oscar was glad he hadn't realized that audience would include his principal. Though he probably should have guessed she had some tie to the hospital since she'd sent him there in the first place. It was weird to think how angry he'd been about it back then, when now he knew he was going to keep coming in, even though his reparations had ended.

"A few weeks ago I recall you telling me you didn't like little kids," she said, the sides of her mouth turning up. "But it certainly seems as though they like you."

"Yeah, they're okay," Oscar said. Though as he glanced up at the stage and saw Freddy's mischievous smile, Henry's round face, and Rosie's eyes shining despite her huge cast, he knew they were more than just okay. They were awesome.

"There were some who weren't so sure of my choice to send you here," Ms. Antonoff went on, her eyes on the kids now, too. "These kids are vulnerable, and they need volunteers who come with big hearts, open hearts. Volunteers who can put their needs second, and the needs of the patients first."

It took Oscar a second to realize she was saying that people thought he was selfish.

"Most sixth graders think of themselves first," Ms. Antonoff said. "They don't want to work hard, and they care more about getting the most baskets themselves instead of passing the ball to get a win for the team."

Oscar winced at that. Apparently he was known for being a ball hog. Though he couldn't really argue with it—he *had* been a ball hog. And as Gabby had already pointed out, he'd been pretty selfish, too.

Ms. Antonoff turned her gaze back to him. "It seems to me, Mr. Madison, that you have learned to share the ball," she said. "And to work hard so that sick kids can have a Festival for the holidays. It seems to me that you were just the right person for this job."

Oscar shrugged, his face growing hot as the principal smiled knowingly at him. Maybe it was true that he liked helping the kids, that being part of a team with Josie and Gabby and Clementine was actually better than thinking about himself all the time. But he wasn't going to just come out and admit that the principal had been right all those weeks ago when she told him he was going to learn a few things. Plus, not *everything* had changed.

"I still don't like Christmas," he told her.

She laughed, then looked up at the activity on the stage. "There's still a bit of time for that to change, too," she told him.

THE REHEARSAL HAD started. Gabby was off to the side of the auditorium with the sibling group, helping them practice. Most of the other kids were with their parents while Josie and Ms. D'Amato helped Dr. Scott and her husband figure out the staging for their act. It was moments like this, when he was alone with nothing to do, that Oscar couldn't ignore the emptiness that carved out his insides. Things his father said, stuff his mother had done, the pile of boxes in the hall that got bigger every day. It threatened to engulf him. He needed to stay with people, to keep busy. Otherwise, it would swallow him whole.

So he headed to the backstage dressing room to see if Ed and Jade were around. The room was empty, but as he turned to leave he saw Josie and Clementine.

"Can I talk to you?" Josie asked, tugging on the sleeve of her dress.

"Sure," Oscar said. The bells on the elf cap he wore for the sing-along rang as he walked toward her. "What's up?"

"I want to give you your Christmas present," Josie said.

This was terrible. Oscar hadn't even thought to get Christmas presents for anyone since he was anti-Christmas and all, but now here he was, the selfish friend again.

"You don't have to give me anything," he said.

"I know," Josie said. "And I know you didn't get me anything, and that's fine. But this is special, and I need you to have it. And if you accept it, it will help me, too."

Now Oscar was intrigued. "Okay," he said.

"Five years ago, I got the best Christmas present of my life," Josie said. She took a deep, shuddering breath, and Oscar suddenly realized there were tears in her eyes. "And now I want to give that gift to you. I want you to have Clementine."

Oscar almost choked; she couldn't be serious.

"My mom and I are moving to an apartment that doesn't allow pets," Josie went on. "We need to find a new home for Clementine. My grandparents are too old to take care of her, and so I want you to have her."

"Why me?" Oscar asked. He still couldn't believe what Josie was saying.

Josie reached down and patted Clementine for a moment. Then she looked up at Oscar. "Because you need her now," she said. "And she knew that. It just took me a little to catch on."

As though she understood Josie's words, Clementine took a step closer to Oscar and leaned against his legs. Oscar knelt down and hugged her close. She was solid and warm, and if he had Clementine with him, he would never be alone. She would be there in the dark of the night when he couldn't sleep, she would stand at his side when his dad left, and she would make his mom smile. Oscar did need that, all of that, so very badly. "Are you sure?" he asked Josie, his voice slightly muffled in Clementine's fur.

"I'm positive," Josie said. She was smiling. "Merry Christmas, Oscar."

THE PARENTS AND backstage helpers were corralling the kids to do a run-through of the sing-along, and Oscar walked over to his mark on the stage, waiting for everyone to be ready. He still couldn't believe that Josie had given him Clementine, but then, as he glanced out at the small group gathered to watch the rehearsal, he saw something even more shocking: Sitting together in the front row were his parents. They were right next to each other, smiling proudly at him. Looking at them you'd never imagine their screaming fights and the fact that they could barely stand being in the same room together. Because right now they looked happy to be sitting next to each other, watching their son about to perform.

Maybe, Oscar thought, his family wasn't completely destroyed. Maybe it was just changing. Yes, it was a change he hated, a change that would be hard. But his parents would still be his parents, and they would still be there for him, even if they were no longer all in the same home.

The whole thing ripped at Oscar, but he had Josie and Gabby, he had Clementine, and he had his parents, too. It would be hard, but, for the first time,

Oscar believed that at some point it would also be okay.

He was no Josie, but when the sing-along began, Oscar got the kids settled and ready, then started the carol and sang his guts out. After all, they were up there to celebrate what was now Oscar's favorite holiday of all.

Chapter 25

Saturday, December 24

The skeleton-Christmas skit had just ended and the lights dimmed. While the X-ray technicians left the stage, Josie made her way to her spot. Her knees were weak as she walked, but she was not alone: Clementine leaned gently against her, reassuring and warm. Clementine was Oscar's dog now, of course. But Josie knew Clementine would always be there, just a few blocks away, whenever Josie needed a furry cuddle. Or a whole lot of courage, like she did right now as she looked out at the auditorium full of what seemed like a thousand people, all sitting and waiting for the next act. Which was her.

Josie's breath was coming in shallow bursts, but she reminded herself to focus on the people who mattered most, the people she wanted to make proud in the next few minutes, under the lights that were about to blaze down bright upon her. She gazed at the place where she had once stood next to her dad lying in a stretcher, beaming as he squeezed her hand before she came up to the stage. He was proud of her already, she could feel it, just like she could feel him here in this room with her. Then there were Gabby and Oscar, who stood just offstage, the two friends who had believed in her before she believed in herself. The friends who saw who Josie was, with and without a costume, and liked what they saw. There in the third row, video camera in hand, was her mom. And next to her were Josie's grandparents, ready to cheer even if Josie just stood there silent. Then there were the kids—Freddy, Melanie, Henry, Alison, and Rosie—waiting to hear her angel song. This was the group Josie sang for. And the other few hundred people? They just happened to be in the room.

The spotlight flickered on, bathing Josie in its golden glow. She took a breath to fill her lungs. Her knees steadied and her hands stilled. She nodded to Jade, who was accompanying her on the piano, and listened as she played the opening chords. The sea of faces looked up at Josie, waiting as the pause came, the moment when it was time, finally, for Josie to sing. So Josie opened her mouth and began, the song pouring out of her, each note radiant and true as Josie sang with her heart and soul.

The applause was thunderous after Josie was done. Her mom was the first to stand, but the mayor was right behind her, and soon the entire auditorium was on its feet, giving Josie a standing ovation.

Josie bowed, then remembered she was in a dress and gave a clumsy curtsy. Clementine barked happily, and Josie knew exactly what the dog was saying.

"Merry Christmas!" Josie cried, her voice carrying over the sound of the applause. "Merry Christmas to you all!"

About the Author

Daphne Benedis-Grab grew up in a small town in Upstate New York, where Christmas was always her favorite holiday. She is the author of *The Angel Tree* and *Alive and Well in Prague, New York*. She has worked a variety of jobs, including building houses for Habitat for Humanity in Georgia, organizing an after-school tutoring program in San Francisco, and teaching ESL in China. She now lives in New York City with her husband, two kids, and a cat, and still looks forward to celebrating Christmas every year. Learn more at www.daphnebg.com.